THE PROPHET'S GAMBIT

Everything's a coincidence.

She heard both phrases in his voice and Aris rocked on her heels, trying to decide which version sounded most like him.

Coming to the shop had been his idea, and yet Lochlen didn't seem all that excited about being here. In fact, he looked almost nervous, standing on the edge of the curb, touching his fingers together.

What did he have to be nervous about? After all, it was *her* parents they were here to learn about, not his. So far, all they'd uncovered was an album devoid of memories and a box full of lies, neither of which did much in the way of helping them find Krysidia. And that was the goal, wasn't it? Learn what they knew and use it to find Krysidia. It's what she thought she wanted, why she'd spent hours scavenging through public records. But now, everything felt heavier: her arms, her eyelids, even her lungs. They were like two sacks of potatoes tethered to a pulley, and every time she wanted a breath, she had to hoist them into the air.

She felt as if the weight of Krysidia lay on her shoulders, that everyone was relying on her mother to know something. But if Krysidia really was this grand haven, if her mother had actually known where it was, wouldn't she still be alive? Aris had voiced this concern to Alek on the car ride over and his answer struck a nerve. "Maybe she didn't want to leave her family," he'd said, and Aris's thoughts had gone straight to Evie. But thinking about her sister only racked her with guilt, so instead, Aris changed tack, hoping to land on a slightly less paralyzing thought; and that was how she ended up thinking about death.

When had her mother realized she was going to die? Was it the moment she turned around? When they plunged into the river? When the car first swerved? The strange thing about death was that, even when you thought you were going to die, you didn't actually *think* you were going to die. After all, every other time you thought you were going to die, you didn't, so why should this time be any different?

Aris glanced down the street, hoping to see Alek on his way back, but caught sight of Mirai bouncing up the sidewalk instead. Well, she heard her before she saw her. Mirai's laugh could fill a theater and have everyone holding out for the reprise. She'd been walking alongside Yuki and Jada, but instantly left them both behind, her hair fluttering as she broke into a jog.

"Saying I missed you would be an understatement," she blurted, drawing Aris in for a hug. "I spent the weekend listening to Yuki spew creation theories while my dad dragged us along on his quest for new carving tools." She pulled away. "I mean, he's my dad and I love him, but that man is painstakingly particular when it comes to chisels." Mirai pressed a hand to her cheek, shaking her head like she just didn't know what she was going to do with him. "But how are you, how's—" Her gaze landed on Lochlen lurking within earshot, and she tugged Aris aside. "How's school?"

Aris raked her fingers through her hair. "Actually, it's all been a bit weird since Alek showed up, but—"

"I'm sorry, he did what?"

"Yeah, I don't know what he was thinking." She picked at one of her curls and attempted to flatten it. "I'm sure he would have gotten in trouble if he wasn't such a history fanatic. Actually, it kind of worked out in my teacher's favor. All Alek had to do was scribble one correct date across the board and half the class was suddenly interested in archeology."

Mirai snorted. "Who knew nerds were so contagious?" She touched the side of Aris's arm, lowering her voice to a whisper. "And the rumors? You know my offer to beat the snot out of that guy still stands."

"About that," Aris mused, her brow dipping as she spoke. "I guess enough people saw Alek and I in the hallway, and now an unsettling number of them actually condone my cheating on Brent." Aris shook her head. "Teenagers are idiots."

Mirai slung an arm around Aris's shoulder and said, "That's exactly what I tell my mother and yet she still expects me to pass calculus." A smile tugged at Aris's lips and as she tucked a piece of hair behind her ear, she noticed a hint of color creep into Mirai's cheeks. A strange chirping noise sounded from overhead and Aris glanced up to see a large black bird circling.

Just then, Alek came trotting up the sidewalk. Aris lit up at the sight of him. "Sorry," he said, scratching the side of his temple. "Parking around here is a mess." He'd barely shoved his keys into his pocket when Mirai descended upon him.

"You," she seethed. "That's where you ran off to on Monday? *Her history class?* You realize that's exactly why I didn't want to tell you." Mirai threw up her hands. "You can't just show up unannounced at her school, doofus. That's borderline stalking."

Alek froze. He opened his mouth as if about to repent, but Mirai didn't give him the chance. As he rubbed the spot above his brow, Aris realized just how much she enjoyed seeing him flustered. He had the face of a boy caught off guard, one who couldn't read energies or anticipate the future. She shot Lochlen a glance just as Jada murmured, "I think he gets it."

With a heavy sigh, Mirai released her shackles and let Jada loop their arm through hers. All six of them were huddled in front of The Twisted Juniper now. Yuki slipped a book into his bag and said, "Are you sure he's legit?"

"No," Lochlen said without hesitation.

Yuki snapped, "Well, maybe we should come back when you are."

"What do you want me to do, go in there and ask to see his crystal? I'd probably get stabbed or something," Lochlen countered dryly.

Yuki raised a hand. "Isn't that why we brought Jada along?"

"Wait, what?" Jada whipped their head around. "You guys didn't say anything about getting stabbed."

Alek shoved his hands in his pockets. "Are we just going to stand out here and snipe at each other all day?" They all turned to look at him.

"Possibly," Lochlen finally said.

Alek rolled his eyes. "You want me to go first?" No one said anything, but everyone cleared the way for him.

Bells chimed overhead as they herded into the tiny shop, and a voice greeted them from behind the counter.

Despite its small size, the store had an enormous selection. Crystals lined the walls, alongside bottled herbs and candles in every color. In the center of the room, little statues were displayed in tall glass cases beside stacks of tinged books and wire-wrapped pendants. On Aris's left was a cabinet full of incense sticks, and the tiny diffuser on display filled the shop with the smell of chamomile.

The shopkeeper stepped out from behind his counter. "Is there anything I can help you—Oh?" He paused. "Twins." Aris looked between Yuki and Mirai, but when she glanced up, it was her the shopkeeper was staring at. He cleared his throat. "Can I help you find something?"

Lochlen's gaze fixed on the storage room door. It creaked open, the gap barely wide enough for a mouse to sneak through. "Yeah," Lochlen said, straightening, "we heard you do spirit readings." The shopkeeper retreated behind his counter and Lochlen threw an article down in front of him.

Aris had already read the clipping: a woman claimed to have made peace with the death of her sister after a gifted medium helped her make contact. Of course, there were plenty of similar stories floating about the internet. Aris had wondered what made this medium so special until she swiped through the article and found a red circle around the word *Reaper*.

Aris thought he'd be older, but he looked to be in his late twenties, just seasoned enough to grow a fully formed beard.

"You should be more careful who you choose to help," Lochlen warned.

The man was so weighed down with bracelets and chains, Aris didn't expect he could straighten as much as he did. She attempted to pick out his crystal, but it was impossible to tell which one was real. He tapped four ring-covered fingers against the glass and said, "I probably shouldn't be talking to a bunch of children then."

Lochlen looked him over and then turned to one of the shelves. He ran a finger over an amethyst cluster. "In your professional opinion," he said in a smooth if not condescending voice, "what's the best way to avoid a ghost?"

The shopkeeper crossed his arms. His eyes narrowed as Lochlen glanced back, but then he raised his chin and said, "Get off the grid."

"And if it's too late for that?"

The shopkeeper smirked. "Run like hell." He relaxed a bit, but Lochlen remained rigid. "Tell me"—the man grinned like it was his turn to play—"can you discern a restless spirit from a docile one?"

"Their eyes," Lochlen said a little too quickly. "The whites of their eyes start to turn gray until eventually—"

"They turn black," the shopkeeper finished.

Aris looked between Lochlen and the medium, waiting for their weird exchange of riddles to be over. It ended up being the shopkeeper who finally conceded defeat, or at least she assumed that's what had happened. The man slouched forward and sighed. "So, have you come seeking a mentor, or are you trying to recruit me for your little teenage army?"

"Neither," Lochlen said plainly, and the shopkeeper stroked the side of his beard. "Try not to look so disappointed." Lochlen looked at Aris, and she promptly reached into her bag. She handed over the photo from the crash, and Lochlen slid it across the table as if it were an illicit substance. "Do you recognize either of the two on the left?"

With one hand still rustling through the wiry hairs on his chin, the shopkeeper studied the image. "I can't say for certain." This time Lochlen turned to Alek, who stepped up to the counter and spread out a handful of bills. The shopkeeper raised his eyebrows. "Car accident, correct?"

"Wait, you've seen them?" Aris pushed in front of Lochlen. "Like"—she swallowed—"as ghosts?"

"I have." He picked up the photograph. "But not for some time now. I'm surprised they hung on for as long as they did. It takes a lot of energy to cling to a life that no longer serves you."

"I'm sure you'd stick around too if you'd been murdered," Lochlen said.

Murdered. Aris hated the word. Her parents had died—that's what she was told, and that's what she said to anyone who asked. Death sounded tragic, sure, but murder sounded nauseating.

The shopkeeper's head tilted as he grimaced. He looked at Lochlen like the boy had accused him of performing the act himself.

"Someone drove them off the road," Aris said, but her voice came out as a whisper, like a pair of wobbly knees threatening to collapse.

The shopkeeper raised his brow as he slid the photo back. "Their accident was tragic, but it was in fact an accident," he said, picking through his necklaces.

Lochlen weaved an arm around Aris and planted his hand on the counter. "Listen, someone was after them. We just want to know who." He craned forward and Aris felt a lock of his hair graze the top of her head. She stilled, mouth pressed into a line as the shopkeeper shifted his attention to a display of tarot cards. "Alek," Lochlen said through clenched teeth. Alek rustled another bill and added it to the pile. "Is there a way to contact them?" Lochlen pressed.

"If they were still around, I'd be able to sense them," the shopkeeper said, his back still turned. He shifted a stack of neatly aligned boxes, making them crooked. "I hope you can find some peace in knowing they've finally moved on."

"No," Aris said, the word choking out of her, and at that the shopkeeper finally turned around.

A weak, knowing smile crossed his lips. "Your parents, right?" Aris nodded. "When a person dies suddenly, they often struggle with acceptance, just like their loved ones. My job is to help them come to terms with their passing before their energy becomes unstable."

Jada picked up a vial of lavender oil and said, "So basically, you're a grief councillor . . . for dead people?" Lochlen shot them a look, and Jada set the bottle back on the shelf.

The shopkeeper resumed picking through his chains, this time the ones on his wrist. "On March 22, at the bridge just west of town, Luke Kalogeras lost control of his car. It had rained that morning and the roads were still slick. His windshield kept fogging up and when he saw a flash of oncoming headlights, he swerved. The car plunged into the river and your parents tried to escape through the window, but neither of them managed to break the glass."

"No," the word came out just as strangled as it did the first time, and Aris shook her head. "My mom got out."

"You're mistaken."

"I'm not mistaken," she bit back. "I saw it."

The shopkeeper's lips parted and his eyes seemed to spark, but only for a second. He rested his arms on the counter, fingers entwined. "Sometimes, we make up stories in an attempt to explain something as unfathomable as an accident. You're trying to direct your grief by looking for someone to blame it on. But the truth is, it wasn't anyone's fault. No one could have saved them. It was simply their time."

Aris wanted to scream. Guilt gutted her, like a knife twisting into her stomach. *An accident, not murder.* Honestly, it was exactly what she'd wanted to hear. To know no one had been after her mother's ring, that she hadn't died just to protect it. But then, hearing the shopkeeper say it out loud . . . everything about the situation felt off.

The man kept his eyes down and said, "I'm sorry I can't be of more help," but Aris was still thinking through details. The ring . . . It had never made sense that her mother had been wearing it in the vision, and maybe that was because it was never a vision in the first place. But that would mean everything she'd seen was just her own twisted imagination: the fear, the desperation, the look in her mother's eyes as she turned around. Mirai reached out a hand, but Aris stepped forward, letting the counter hold the weight she could no longer bear.

"But then—what about the album?" Aris was muttering more to herself than anyone when a sharp crack of thunder commanded the room's attention. Seven heads turned in unison as one of the display cases exploded in front of them. A million tiny shards of glass collected like freshly fallen snow at its base and then, out of the corner of her eye, Aris caught the flutter of something purple. She whipped her head around, tracking the movement as if it were a fly buzzing around the room. Whatever it was, it lingered for a moment in gentle swirls. "Mom?"

"What?" Mirai murmured.

"She's here, I can feel her," Aris said quickly—and then she wasn't. The surrounding air changed, and Aris bolted out of the shop. She tore down the sidewalk purely on instinct. Chasing something she couldn't even see.

It has to be her, Aris thought. *She wouldn't have held on as long as she did just to give up. There has to be a reason.* Thunder roared again, louder than she'd ever heard. Even if it was just an accident, Aris still had questions about her family, about her powers. She paused. The feeling was fading. She whipped her head around, looking for a sign. There was a slight ripple in the air and Aris turned to chase it as a gust of wind threatened to steal her coat. She barely had one foot on the road when someone yanked her back.

"What the hell are you doing? I'm gonna lose her." Aris fought the arm that held her. "There aren't even any cars—" A dark gray SUV came whipping around the corner, its tires screeching as it veered onto the road in front of her. Her legs went numb. She had tears in her eyes, but she held them there, let them pool until her vision completely flooded. The sky continued grumbling, but it sounded farther away. Finally, she dropped her hands, surrendering to the body now cradling her, to the pair of arms, one slung across her shoulders and the other around her waist.

"You sure do cry a lot," Lochlen said, relaxing his grip.

When Aris looked up at him, two droplets raced down either side of her cheek and she choked her way through a laugh as she wiped them with her sleeve. "Only since meeting you," she sniffled.

Lochlen set a hand on her head and sighed. "Didn't I say your thoughtlessness would be your undoing?" The small noise he made next almost sounded like a laugh, and Aris couldn't help but wonder if she actually had been hit by that SUV.

When Lochlen went silent, Aris turned to see Alek had caught up with them. As he slowed to a halt, she and Lochlen scrambled to opposite ends of the sidewalk. She wiped her cheeks again and then glanced up to see Alek looking as if he'd been struck across the face. Her cheeks burned and so did the back of her throat. Alek rushed to her side. "What did you do?" he exclaimed, glaring at Lochlen.

"Your job, apparently," Lochlen chided. "She'd have been flattened by a car if I hadn't grabbed her."

"Like you're one to talk."

Lochlen took a step toward Alek. "What's that supposed to mean?"

"You claim that you taught her to read photos, didn't you? Just look how that turned out."

The blood drained from Aris's face. They were arguing again. About her, *again*.

"You don't know anything, okay," Lochlen snapped.

"I know you've been against her from the beginning. You didn't think we could trust her, and now apparently everything you taught her was a lie. Am I supposed to believe that's some sort of coincidence?"

Nothing's a coincidence, Aris thought again. *Everything's a coincidence.* She slowly sank to the ground. She'd done nothing but cause problems. She didn't know how to help them find Krysidia. She didn't know how to protect herself. She didn't even know how to use her magic. And now they were fighting over whom to blame.

Me, Aris thought. *I'm to blame.*

Blame me . . .

Blame me . . .

Please . . . just . . . stop . . .

Aris pressed a hand to her head.

Lochlen curled a finger and jabbed it in Alek's direction as if he couldn't fully commit to pointing. "You know, you're the one who didn't want me teaching her in the first place." His action almost looked more threatening than mere pointing, the way a scimitar could be more intimidating than a long sword.

A warm arm scooped her up and Aris looked up to see Mirai crouched beside her.

Alek brushed a hand through his hair. "Sure, I'm the monster because I didn't want her first vision to be of the moment her parents stopped breathing." Lochlen said nothing at this, instead staring at Alek, his mouth slightly parted. "Her parents are dead," Alek continued in a low grumble. "She doesn't know who killed them or if anyone even killed them at all. The least you could do is show a bit of fucking sympathy."

Lochlen narrowed his eyes, any trace of guilt vanishing from his features. He closed the gap between them, and, with a voice too loud to be a whisper, he said, "Is that what you were doing in the mountains? Showing her *a bit of sympathy*?"

Aris was watching Alek and what looked like the edge of a shadow flickering behind him. She raised a finger to warn him, but—

"This isn't about either of you," Mirai screamed in a ragged voice.

The next thing Aris knew, Alek was kneeling in front of her. He unscrewed the cap of a water bottle and held the bottle up to her lips.

Ghosts were supposed to feel cold. At least, that's what all the stories claimed. But when that case shattered, Aris's cheeks had flushed. She'd felt anger, frustration. Almost like she was sitting too close to an open flame.

Water dribbled down the side of her mouth as she drank. As hard as she tried, she couldn't keep her hand steady. It felt like someone was shaking her, telling her to wake up. Maybe this was all one long dream.

Alek.

His friends.

Her ring.

Maybe she'd blink and find herself alone in her bedroom.

Aris almost gave herself a headache trying to keep her eyes open. When she finally gave in, she kept them closed. Because as ridiculous as this whole dream was, she didn't want to wake up. She wasn't ready to go back to the life she had before.

"She's not hurt, is she?"

"Someone just get her up before we start attracting attention."

"Relax, okay? She's been through a lot."

Aris.

Aris, open your eyes.

There was a voice in her head again and, even worse, it was trying to tell her what to do. *Five more minutes*, she thought back, as if throwing the covers up over her head.

Something cold trickled down her back and Aris jumped to her feet, eyes blazing. She whipped around to see Lochlen holding the water bottle from earlier, only now it was empty. "I cannot believe you just did that," she huffed.

"It worked, didn't it?" Lochlen said. "You can't just take a nap in the middle of the sidewalk, for fuck's sake. We're downtown."

"I wasn't taking a nap," Aris snapped. "I was—" She blinked at him, having only just processed Alek's words: *I know you've been against her from the beginning.* "I don't know." She wrapped both hands around the back of her neck and took a brief survey of her surroundings. She would've needed both hands to count the number of banks alone, and the shop should've looked out of place by comparison, but for some reason, it was almost the opposite. She glanced back at their little circle. They were all staring at her. Mirai, like she thought Aris had lost her mind, Jada, like they were offering to help her find it, and Yuki, like he wasn't all that surprised. Then there was Alek. Alek wasn't staring *at* her so much as he was staring *through* her.

"Back at the shop," Mirai said, as if tiptoeing. "You said you felt your mom?"

Aris took a hurried breath. "Yeah, I don't know, maybe. Or maybe I just jumped to conclusions. I thought I could feel her"—she shrugged—"but I also thought I'd been able to read that license plate." Aris pressed her hands to her cheeks and took a seat on the curb. "Turns out it was all in my head."

Mirai sat down beside her and pulled a packet of fruit snacks from her jacket pocket. She had only just placed it in Aris's hand when Lochlen took several steps toward the shop and said, "He lied." Five heads turned just as quickly as they had at the sound of shattering glass, and as lightheaded as she was, Aris didn't dare reach for the gummies. Lochlen continued. "When I touched the license plate, I watched them get run off the road. I saw your mother come up for air and then"—he took an unsteady breath—"I saw a hand dunk her under until . . ." He cleared his throat. "It wasn't an accident."

Aris closed her hand over the wrapper and listened to it crinkle. "But then why—"

"I wanted to test the extent of your powers." He dragged a foot across the concrete.

Alek had been standing an awkward distance away, but Aris could still see the tension build in his shoulders. "You mean you knew what happened, and you made her watch it anyway?" His words came out like a knife whittling the tip of a spear, and his fists were clenched as if he were actually holding a blade. The way they were positioned reminded Aris of how Mirai had held her katana, but what Alek wielded was much scarier than that.

Yuki and Jada both straightened.

"It's okay," Aris said. "It's not like he forced me."

Alek scowled. "No, he just made you think you were the only option."

She thought about the license plate and how it was lying on the rocks. How the last thing she had seen was her mother's eyes go wide. How it felt as if a plug had been pulled . . . Aris realized it was the plate being ripped from her hands. She looked to Lochlen, but he avoided her gaze.

"I didn't expect you to see anything," Lochlen admitted, his hands tucked away. "You only just found out about your powers. I thought maybe you'd latch onto a feeling. I never imagined you'd be able to see the whole bloody accident." His mouth twisted. "Honestly"—he met her gaze—"I was mildly impressed."

Aris didn't know what to make of his confession. After all, he was still the guy who offered her poisoned tea. So she got to her feet and brushed the street dust from her jeans. She looked beyond him to The Twisted Juniper and said, "Why do you think he lied?"

"Either he's protecting someone," Lochlen breathed, "or he's working for them." He touched his fingers together again, a gesture Aris now recognized as a nervous tic. "I got this feeling back at the shop. Like maybe we weren't the only ones there." He glanced at his watch. "I think this was a setup."

"And you're just telling us this now?" Yuki barked.

Lochlen looked almost ethereal with his eyes glossed over. He'd stopped moving altogether, and Aris had the sudden urge to reach for him. "Whoever they were, they're gone now," he clarified. "I'm pretty sure her mom scared them off."

"How the hell can a prophet get lured into a setup?" Yuki sneered, and at that Aris opened the bag of fruit snacks and dumped the whole thing in her mouth. She was still chewing when she realized Yuki's comment had been directed at Lochlen.

"I-I wasn't thinking."

"No shit, you weren't thinking."

Mirai reached up and grabbed the hem of Yuki's shirt. "Whoa, hey, let's just calm down a minute."

"I will not calm down," Yuki said. "You know what this means, don't you?"

Mirai dropped her hand. "How long do you think we have?"

"A couple weeks, at best."

Lochlen took another step toward The Twisted Juniper and she realized he didn't have his tarot cards. She could see the side of his hand as it trembled. This wasn't a dream. This was real. All of them were real. And they had been lured here by someone. *Someone who knew about her mother.*

But despite everything that had just happened, what shocked her the most was seeing Alek walk over and put a hand on Lochlen's shoulder, as if they hadn't just been screaming at each other five minutes ago. "Everything's going to be fine," Alek said, but Aris had a sinking suspicion he was the only one who actually believed that.

When she turned back to the shop, something was moving in the window and for a split second she thought they were being watched. She waited, expecting to see the shopkeeper glaring back, but the sign on the door simply flipped from open to closed, and then everything stilled.

CHAPTER 20

When Garret said he found Braxton, Harrison was hoping for an address, not a circle on a map. Especially not one with a six-block radius. They drove around a neighborhood neither of them was familiar with while Garret shouted out impulsive instructions.

Left here. Right there. Another left. Wait, no, circle around again.

Just when Harrison was getting frustrated with the spontaneity, Garret told him to pull over.

The street was poorly lit and lined with shops about to close, the largest of which was a café at the end of the block. "You're sure he's in there?" Harrison asked, his head craned all the way back.

"Like, 87 percent sure," Garret said, one hand clasping the annotated copy of *Dream of the Red Chamber* Braxton had sent Harrison for his high school graduation. He'd hoped the handwritten notes Brax had scribbled throughout the margins would be enough for Garret to track him down, but apparently the best the boy could do was make an arbitrary guess.

Garret released his seatbelt and reached for the door, but Harrison stuck out a hand. "You'd better wait here." He took another look at the café and double checked that the cash he'd scrounged up was still in his pocket. His plan was simple. Or at least it would be if everything went perfectly. But already, things had begun gravitating out of line. He'd intended to come alone. He'd assumed Garret would be able to hand him a slip of paper with an address on it, and he'd figured that address would lead him to either an apartment building or a tavern. But so far, none of these expectations had been accurate.

He locked the car, just in case Garret's surmise turned out to be more fortuitous than his own, but the closer Harrison got to the end of the block, the faster his hope dissolved. He'd known Brax for a long time, and if there was one thing he knew for certain, it was that the man had extravagant taste—and while the building in front of him was quaint, it definitely wasn't flashy.

In the end, it was curiosity more than anything that got his foot in the door and when he stepped inside, the café smelled not of coffee but of something else. It was an intense odor—a cross between damp wood chips and lemon-scented hand sanitizer. The table legs in the café were wrapped in twine and shelves fashioned like steps led up to a perch near the ceiling. Something brushed up against his leg and a tickle formed in his nose. Harrison looked down at a large pair of green eyes belonging to a lumpy orange cat.

Garret must've been mistaken—Harrison's heart sank a little—Brax definitely wasn't here. The only table that wasn't empty had a pair of elderly ladies chatting away, each with a Persian purring on their lap. Even if Brax had resorted to working as a barista in a place like this . . . well, if that were the case, then he probably wouldn't be of much help.

"What can I get you?" someone called out from behind the bar. Harrison bit down on his tongue as he turned, but the face behind the counter was unfamiliar.

He ordered a coffee to go, mostly because he felt awkward leaving empty-handed, but as he made for the door, a man with bright red hair blew past him. Turning on his heel, Harrison asked the barista for another splash of cream as the man's flaming head disappeared behind a door labeled "employees only," and then, with both hands planted on the counter, Harrison leaned forward just enough to see a staircase draped in rich, wine-colored velvet. The barista cleared his throat, and Harrison staggered back, his cheeks turning a pale shade of pink as the man held out his cup. But when Harrison went to grab it, the barista waited an extra second before letting go, giving Harrison a cautionary look, the kind that was both a question and a warning—but primarily the latter. Forcing a smile, Harrison thanked the man again and pulled out his phone, pretending to check his voicemail.

One long sip and a quick text later, the café's phone rang.

"Yes, sir, I understand," he heard the barista say. "Yes, I'm looking at the date right now. No, well—Yes, of course, sir, just give me a moment." The worker fled to the kitchen and Harrison quickly dumped his coffee before slipping across the room. The smell of incense wafted down to meet him as he opened the door, and all he could see was a soft glow at the top of the staircase.

He took a long, quiet breath before braving the first step, but something brushed between his legs before he could plant his foot. Harrison pressed one hand to his racing heart and the other to his mouth to keep from squeaking as the lumpy orange cat trotted leisurely past him. He took another shaky breath as its tail disappeared around the corner.

If the cat hadn't already announced his entrance, the floorboards certainly did. They creaked beneath his feet, the sound getting higher with every step, as if he was climbing up the keys of a grand piano. It wasn't until he reached the end of the staircase that he realized just how terrible his plan was. He was hovering a few inches below the foot of a banister when his knees locked up. They, for one, weren't eager to find out what was waiting around that corner.

Less than a second later, a dart whizzed past his nose, confirming that yes, this was, in fact, a terrible plan. He looked to where the end of the dart protruded from the edge of a tapestry, but perhaps what he should have been focusing on was the girl who'd thrown it.

The orange cat stretched out beside her feet, licking its lips as if it had just caught a mouse, and Harrison was worried that was exactly what had happened. He took a step back. "Sorry," he rushed to say, grabbing hold of the railing. "I thought this was the bathroom."

The girl's eyes turned to ice as she cocked her head. "Why don't I believe you?" she said in a honeyed voice.

He tried to swallow a sneeze, and it came out almost like a whimper. He thought about running, but something told him that was exactly what she was hoping for. Instead, he took another step back, his heel teetering on the edge of the stair as he choked out Braxton's name. Her eyes narrowed and she charged forward, slamming him against the wall. "Who are you?" she seethed. "What do you want with Brax?"

"Daven—Dave—Da—"

"What the hell is going on down there?" a voice called from through the banister, and then, like an angel peeking down from its cloud, Braxton stuck his head out and said, "Davenport? Is that you?" He waved a hand. "That's enough, Kayla, he's cool."

With a pout, the girl released her grip, and Harrison toppled over, gasping. He watched her slink back up the steps. She couldn't have been much older than seventeen, and his stomach churned at the thought. What the hell was Brax thinking? Recruiting a child to do his bidding—Harrison swallowed a lump in his throat, realizing he had done the same thing with Garret. The would-be bruising along his neck suddenly felt warranted as he made his way into the room.

There were at least twice as many cats upstairs as he'd seen in the café. They stretched out their paws on stained cushions and curled up along a trio of overlapping rugs. The girl, Kayla, kept her eyes glued to him as he inched toward a large round table. "How's your brother?" Braxton asked, not bothering to introduce Harrison to either of the two men beside him.

Harrison shoved his hands into the pockets of his beige coat. "I don't know," he said in a small voice. "I haven't heard from him since he took off." Honestly, he thought Brax more than anyone would've known where he was. In fact, Harrison had half expected to find Elias sitting in one of the leather armchairs he'd passed on his way over.

Braxton nudged an empty chair with his foot, his smile faltering. He snuck a peek at the cards pressed against his hand and threw a handful of chips into the center of the table. Of the men on either side of him, one added to the pile, and the other tossed his hand.

Elias had been running with Brax for as long as Harrison could remember, but back then, it was mostly just the two of them. They seemed to make decent money hiring themselves out for high-risk jobs. Elias had been just sixteen when he surprised Harrison with a first edition of *The Lion, the Witch, and the Wardrobe*. To this day, that copy was still the most valuable thing he owned. Harrison had been too young to know what type of jobs they'd been—only that after Aleksander was born, Stephen had used them to fight Elias for custody, and he'd won.

After that, Elias had tried to distance himself from Brax, but his partner hadn't been keen to let him go. Brax had wanted to start a different kind of business at that point, and Harrison could still remember Elias's face when Brax first suggested the idea. He'd been eavesdropping on the two of them through a basement window at the time; Elias had a cigarette in his hand and nearly coughed up a lung before letting out a string of curse words, most of which Harrison had learned that night.

Harrison took a seat across the table as the two men flipped their hands. Brax smirked and silently collected his winnings. *This really is a horrendous plan*, Harrison thought, watching Brax build up a tower of orange chips. *Why on earth did I think I could just waltz in here and*—Braxton looked up at him, eyes sparkling, and heat flashed through Harrison.

With a resigned expression, Harrison slid a wad of cash across the table. Braxton flicked his gaze over the money as he straightened the deck of cards and then, with a nod, he dismissed his mates.

"I need a crystal," Harrison said in what he thought was his tough voice, which, as it turned out, was really just his teacher voice. The orange cat jumped onto the table and brushed its tail against Harrison's face. He reached up to rub his eye and then thought better of it.

"His name is Helios," Brax said, his fingers vanishing into its thick orange fur. "The guy who owns this place is a familiar, so he never turns away a stray."

Familiar. Harrison always found it interesting how words got twisted and reused by people who made assumptions rather than asking questions. If you asked most people nowadays, they'd tell you a familiar was an animal that could talk to humans; little did they know it was actually the opposite. Compared to someone who couldn't be injured, communicating with animals seemed inferior, but familiars could be quite dangerous. After all, animals made excellent spies.

When Helios rolled over, Brax reached out to scratch his belly, and the cat latched onto his arm. One second it was kicking its feet against his elbow and the next it was licking his wrist. When it finally hopped down, Harrison's glance went right to Brax's arm. *Not a single claw mark.*

When Brax let out a sigh, Harrison straightened. He didn't know exactly how long the two of them had sat in silence, only that when Brax finally slid the cash back, it felt as if he'd been hit by an anvil.

Braxton hadn't bothered counting it. He hadn't even taken the elastic off to see if Harrison had put the biggest bills on the outside, which he had. Harrison had tried it both ways: big bills out, big bills in. He'd even tried alternating them.

$23,578. He'd counted it at least thirteen times. It was everything from his savings plus his retirement fund, and he'd had to make up a story about buying a used car to convince the bank to let him take it all out at once. At first, it seemed like a lot of money, but by the ninth or tenth time through, it had lost all meaning.

"I could sell my car," he pleaded, his stomach tightening. "And-and-and I've got a couple of first edition books. Maybe if I—"

"You know I'd help you out if I could." Brax's voice was solemn. "But it's not just me anymore. I've got guys to pay and half a dozen clients ready to bid." He dragged a hand along his jaw. "And, of course, our last retrieval didn't exactly go as planned . . ." Braxton trailed off and for the first time, Kayla turned away. There was something about the word *retrieval* that made his insides knot together. For all he knew, it could've been one of Brax's guys who put Garret's mother in a wheelchair. "Look, it doesn't matter," Brax continued with a huff. "My point is, the crystals we curate go for a hundred times what you've got."

Harrison heard the words as if they were muffled, as if time had slowed and his mind was racing to catch up. By the time it finally did, he felt painfully small. His skin was crawling—crawling to get away from this place, these people, to never be seen again. His stomach was gnawing at itself, eager to dissolve, to disappear, to stop existing. He'd damn near thrown himself at Braxton's feet and the man had shucked him off the way a king might decline to help a starving peasant. But what hurt the most was his heart finally breaking; it broke for the boy who had once worshipped Brax like a prince, because in this moment, Harrison knew he would never be worthy of the man in front of him. Brax tilted his head. "You understand, right?" The words were a final thunk to his head, and for the second time that evening, Harrison forced a smile.

He understood, alright. He understood how naïve he'd been for coming here, for thinking something would work out in his favor for once. He understood that deep down he was still Elias's dorky kid sibling, asking to tag along on his brother's next job, and Brax was still offering him a heartfelt grin and telling him to wait until he was older. And it didn't matter that Harrison was twenty-eight because the type of *older* Brax was referring to had nothing to do with age.

Harrison held back a sigh as he tucked the measly stack of bills back into his pocket and pushed up from the table. His father once told him that being born a protector meant he'd lived virtuously in a past incarnation. But what was the point of depriving himself in a previous life if he couldn't even access his powers in this one?

It felt as if the universe was messing with him. Karma had taken all his faith and forgotten to pay him back, and it was a lot like lending a stranger your phone and then watching them run off with it. At first, you'd be angry at the thief for being cruel, but after a while you'd realize you let yourself get tricked.

Harrison doubted Brax ever got tricked. He doubted he believed in karma. He doubted he even believed in Llewellyn. And yet, *he* had everything. He had jewel-encrusted pillows, for god's sake. This time, when Harrison glanced back at Brax, it wasn't an angel he saw staring down at him; it was a devil peering up.

He knew Brax wasn't a good person, but at least he wasn't a fool.

Tonight was the night.

Tonight was the night Harrison Davenport finally grew up.

Braxton quirked his lips as Harrison placed both hands on the table and said, "What if I told you I knew the whereabouts of two Anathemians?"

Brax dropped his chin, looking Harrison over as if trying to read his hand. "I would say you have my attention."

Harrison rushed to add that the Anathemians were young and probably hadn't mastered their powers yet. Honestly, a small piece of him was hoping Brax would stop him there, that he would say he didn't go after children, and that just a smidgen of Harrison's faith would be restored. But instead, Braxton perked up in his chair, and with a snap of his fingers, one of his men appeared beside him with a pipe. "Well done, Little D," he said and blew out a cloud of smoke. "Who would've guessed you'd turn out even ballsier than your brother."

Little D. That was perhaps the worst nickname on the planet. It had been bad enough in his teenage years, but now it just seemed wrong. This time, he put up with it for fear of pissing the guy off. But once, Harrison had been happy to have a nickname at all, no matter how stupid. Because it came from *him*. Brax must've been in his late thirties by now, but he looked the same as he always had. Same messy blond hair, a touch darker than his skin. Same perfectly trimmed scruff. *Same piercing blue eyes . . .*

A cough threatened to rise in Harrison's lungs as he inhaled whatever Brax had passed him, but he swallowed it down, trying not to think about all the lives he was about to destroy. Trying not to think about how horrible it felt to finally grow up.

CHAPTER 21

"What is *she* doing here?" Yuki griped, sliding into the backseat of Alek's car.

Aris bit back a groan.

Alek glared at Yuki's reflection in the rearview mirror. "You know, meeting her is what triggered the tarot card to change in the first place. Or don't you remember?" Alek nodded to where Aris sat in the passenger seat. "She might even be more helpful than you."

Yuki rolled his eyes. "I seriously doubt that."

Aris had to admire his honesty, if nothing else. Alek looked at her, eyes dipping apologetically, but she waved it off. She was getting used to Yuki's jabs. Besides, Alek couldn't protect her from everything, although no doubt he tried.

He'd offered to drive her to school this morning, and she had to promise to text him when she got to her locker just to keep him from following her to class again. She told him she'd be fine, that despite what happened at the shop, she was a prophet and she could anticipate things before they went awry. But the truth was she couldn't stop thinking about what Lochlen had said: *I got this feeling, like maybe we weren't the only ones there.* Aris hadn't gotten that feeling. Or even an inkling. Just like she hadn't realized the tea Lochlen concocted was toxic, not until it was right beneath her nose. If Alek knew just how terrible her instincts were, he'd probably stop sleeping altogether.

She had spent the first half of the school day worried she was being too paranoid, and the second half worried she wasn't paranoid enough. Even now that school was over and she was back with Alek, she still couldn't make up her mind. The world around them seemed normal enough. Then again, Aris wasn't the best judge of normal, and the three of them *were* on their way to find information on a mythical realm their ancestors may or may not have been banished from.

When they arrived at the university library, the first thing Aris noticed was a boarded-up window on the second floor. A police car was stationed out front, although the officer behind the wheel appeared to be working on a crossword puzzle.

For a moment, she worried they'd have to come back another day, but nobody stopped them from walking through the set of heavy wooden doors at the front of the building. When they got inside, Yuki took the lead, weaving through marble columns and dark oak desks. Security guards were stationed throughout the room, and as Aris stopped to admire a case claiming to hold a collection of notes from one of Hypatia's disciples, she received several glances. Alek touched a hand to her arm, moving her along.

He and Yuki led her down a dimly lit hallway labeled "IV" and she found herself in what looked like an old-fashioned study. Wooden shelves lined the back wall, and a small sitting area was shoved beside a set of stairs. On the other side of the room was a large antique desk and a round-looking man with red hair and a smattering of facial piercings. "Not really a good time, guys," he said from behind the counter.

Yuki surveyed the room. The couch and chairs were both empty, and no one had followed them down the hall. "What happened?" he asked in a hushed voice.

"There was a break-in last night." The man leaned forward, resting his elbows beside his computer. "A couple of guards were injured, but nothing too serious."

Yuki seemed fixated on the cuff of his sleeve as he said, "I'm guessing they still haven't caught the guy?"

"According to the report, the two guards in the hospital radioed to say they had the suspect surrounded, but when they woke up, they both said the same thing—that the last thing they remember was struggling to breathe."

"Seems extreme for a library," Alek added.

Yuki crossed his arms. "What did they take?"

The man hesitated. "They're still taking inventory."

"What is it?" Yuki pressed, his eyes flicking between the man and the door behind his desk.

"So far, the only thing unaccounted for is one of your mom's theses. She's already been notified, of course." Yuki wiped a hand across his face and the man lowered his eyes. "I also happened to notice her transfer request. I hope it's not because of the break-in."

When Yuki dropped his hand, he suddenly had Mirai's soft cheeks. "Actually, my father's line of work is quite specialized, and there isn't enough business in Elsley. My parents have been browsing houses in a few bigger cities for some time now." He let out a small laugh. "Perhaps the assailant was bitter about her departure."

The man rubbed a hand along his chin and Aris heard the rustle of stubble against dry skin. His mouth quirked as he considered Yuki's statement. "That's actually why I'm here," Yuki continued. "I don't know how much longer we'll be in town. In fact, this might be my last chance to visit the library."

The man lowered his hand onto the desk and scanned the room. "Okay," he whispered. "Just be quick." He pulled out a brass key and unlocked the door behind his desk. He held it open with his foot and Alek signaled for Aris to follow as he and Yuki snuck inside.

The mysterious locked room was just large enough to fit a square desk and four chairs within the constraints of three narrow rows of shelves. "He seems nice," Aris said as the door clicked shut.

Yuki blew past her and threw his bag down on one of the chairs. "Yes, well, that's what happens when you pay people well enough. Right, Alek?"

Aris smirked. "Maybe he should start paying you."

Yuki shot her a look before disappearing behind the shelf. There was a mix of books and files on the shelves, all mingled beneath headings printed onto thin strips of paper: Ancient Religion, Paranormal Sightings, Midcentury Witchcraft. Some sections were tiny, and others took up entire shelves. She turned back to Alek. "What exactly is this place?"

Alek took a seat in one of the wooden chairs. "Elsley has an abnormally high rate of missing persons. That, combined with unusual weather patterns and the occasional animal attack, makes it something of a hot spot for supernatural research."

Aris joined him across the table. "The university actually funds that type of stuff?"

"Funds it, yes. But I doubt they'd ever actually publish anything. With paranormal theories, nobody wants to be first to say it, but everyone wants to be second." He tapped a finger against the table. "It's only accessible to university professors." Alek tipped his head. "And us."

Us. Alek wasn't just referring to the three of them, but to the others as well—to Mirai and Jada and Lochlen. To the friends he'd known for half his life. "Well, okay." Aris shot to her feet. "Where do we start?"

"You can start by keeping your mouth shut," Yuki said through an empty slot in the shelf. "My parents have given me until the next full moon to find something worthwhile, and I need to concentrate."

Aris straightened. "That's in five days."

"I'm well aware." Yuki retorted. "Thanks to you, our chances of survival in this town have significantly diminished."

Alek raked a hand through his hair. "It's not her fault."

"You're right, it's *yours*. I told you she would get us all killed, and you refused to listen." At that, Yuki vanished again.

"She deserved to know the truth about her powers."

"And what about me?" Yuki demanded, his voice an echo from beyond the books. "Did I deserve to waste half my life chasing Krysidia?

Handwriting thousands of pages to avoid being traced, meticulously covering up my findings, only to have it all ripped away by the recklessness of one girl?"

Aris knew Yuki was only lashing out because he was scared; it was just as Mirai had said. But it still wasn't exactly fun listening to him blame her for everything. He oozed resentment and took every opportunity to batter her with it, as if he was egging a car. Aris sighed. He had to run out of ammunition eventually, right?

"For the last time, it wasn't her fault." Alek blew out a breath. "Lochlen made a mistake—"

"Lochlen hasn't been himself since she showed up," Yuki countered, re-emerging with a stack of files. "Don't pretend like you haven't noticed."

Aris was still trying to figure out what Lochlen's true self must be like when Alek got to his feet and drew back an arm. She was so sure he was about to punch Yuki in the face when a cascade of bills launched out of his hand like a confetti cannon. Yuki closed his eyes as money rained down around him. He looked down at the mess of bills and opened his mouth. "Ah." Alek raised a finger. "You have to be nicer now."

Yuki frowned. "Very cute."

"Would you look at that? It actually worked." Alek gave Aris an approving nod and then turned back to Yuki, arms crossed. "Now, I believe Aris asked where you wanted her to start."

"Fine," Yuki said begrudgingly. "Just bring me anything that mentions meridians and how to find them."

"Meridians." Aris nodded. "Got it." She took a step toward the shelves before turning on her heel. "What's a meridian?"

Yuki scoffed. "I told you she wouldn't be of much help."

Alek stretched out a welcoming hand, and Aris sat back down. He drew an X in the thick layer of dust coating the table. "A meridian is a spot where multiple ley lines intersect to form a greater concentration of power."

"Ley lines . . . like at the ruins?" She remembered something Lochlen mentioned about her powers being stronger there.

Yuki flipped open one of his files. "'Electro-magnetic currents create unique frequencies that can distort sound as well as light,'" he read aloud. "'For this reason, it is suspected that the concentration of ghost sightings at specific locations are due to hallucinations rather than supernatural activity.'"

"Oh," Aris said. "Well, have you—"

"Yes." Yuki flipped open a new document. "I've mapped the most popular locations, but the ghost sightings don't follow an obvious line." He tossed the second document in what looked like a discard pile and began reading a third. "While that may not help us locate the ley line, it does reinforce the theory that Elsley is built around a meridian."

Aris reached for his pile of rejects, pausing to rub her eyes. She was tired in a way that sleep alone couldn't cure. But she'd also just learned her mom spent twelve years clinging to life as a ghost. Which, by comparison, made Aris feel utterly pathetic. "And finding this meridian will help us find Krysidia?" she asked, skimming through a table of contents.

Alek and Yuki shared a glance, and then Alek scooted his chair until he and Aris shared a corner. "Have you ever taken a yoga class?"

Aris set the file down slowly. "At school, yeah." She looked between the two boys. "Why?"

Alek leaned his head against his hand. "You know all that stuff they tell you, like focusing your energy in the soles of your feet?" Aris nodded. "Right, so what they're actually referring to is your energy network. Basically, we're made up of a series of paths for energy to flow between." He paused just long enough for her to request clarification or argue with one of his statements. Aris did neither. "The theory is," Alek continued, "every time these paths intersect, it creates a focal point for harboring energy. So when an instructor says to focus your energy in your soles, they're actually telling you to divert energy from other focal points to the ones in your feet."

Alek folded his arms as he sat up straight. "Now here's where things get interesting." He smirked. "Theoretically, the earth itself could be considered its own entity, which means it has a network of its own."

"So ley lines are just—"

"Energy currents resonating deep within the earth." He drew two circles in the thick layer of dust coating the table. "Now, if we can move the energy within our own systems, it stands to reason that the earth can do the same. And if we ourselves are made up of energy, then the earth could use its network to send us from one point to another." He added a line connecting the two circles.

Aris took a breath. "So, when you say *meridian*, you actually mean—"

"Portal."

"How did you think we were getting to Krysidia?" Yuki chirped. "A magic school bus? Or maybe we'd all go diving through barriers at a train platform?" He crossed his arms and smirked. "I've got a wardrobe I can shove you in, if you'd like."

Aris cocked her head. "How is any of that different from what we're looking for?" She leaned sideways in her chair, trying to meet Yuki's gaze. "Technically, they're all portals too, aren't they?"

The corner of Alek's mouth curled. "She's got you there."

"She hasn't *got* me anywhere, okay? My *point* is, whatever we're looking for is a natural phenomenon. It's going to be highly unpredictable. We can't just go barging in like idiots." Yuki discarded the last of his files. "Meridians exist all over the world. Not only do we have to find one, but we have to find the *right* one."

"How did you find the ruins?" Aris asked.

Yuki paused. "Accidentally."

"Couldn't you just follow the ley line from there?"

"We could." Yuki crossed his arms again. "If we knew which direction it went. But without a second point to go off, it's pretty hopeless."

"Have you tried using a dowsing rod?" Aris hadn't known the words *ley line*, but she'd read a story once about a mystic using a pair of twigs to map out dragon currents, which, after Alek's explanation, she realized might actually be the same thing.

Yuki snorted. He was tucking the files under his arm when he noticed Aris blinking at him. "Oh, you're serious?"

Her expression flattened. "So we're gonna sit here talking about portals taking us to hidden realms, but dowsing rods are a ridiculous suggestion?"

"Yes."

Aris frowned. Dowsing rods were no more ridiculous than tarot cards. She shrank into her chair. Yuki returned to the shelves with his pile and Aris began picking at her nails. "If the portal relies on the same energy as the ruins, does that mean it's invisible as well? And that only Anathemians can use it?"

There was a tinge of sadness in Yuki's voice as he said, "The only ones who will be going through are those of us with crystals."

"But—" *Evie.*

"A meridian is an energy junction, which means trying to navigate it is not just difficult, but incredibly dangerous. Think of it like trying to hold together a bridge and cross it at the same time. The energy in our crystals acts as a stabilizer."

"How do you know so much about a place we're not even sure exists?" Aris asked what she thought was an innocent question.

"Oh, I don't know," Yuki drawled, "maybe the last eight years of research I've done. Or the thirty years my mother did before that."

She stared up and off to the side. "So you've done thirty-eight years of research and still haven't found anything—" Aris threw a hand over her mouth. Alek's eyes went wide and she could see him struggling to keep his jaw from dropping as he picked up one of the bills and slowly slid it toward her. When Yuki came around the corner, it was like something out of a horror movie. His eyes weren't wide like Alek's—they were bulging. He looked like he might explode as Aris scrambled to apologize. It was three or four bouts of "I'm sorry" and "I didn't mean it" and "That came out wrong" before she found the rest of her words. "I just find it hard to believe your mom would put so much work into finding Krysidia just to leave it all behind."

Yuki returned to his chair, and Aris scooted closer to Alek. "You really don't get it, do you?" he said, although he didn't sound nearly as angry as he had looked a minute ago. If anything, he actually sounded concerned.

"Lochlen said we weren't alone. He said your mom's spirit scared them off, which means if she hadn't, there's a very good chance we'd already be dead. Obviously, the shopkeeper was just the distraction. He was likely stalling while someone else prepared to ambush us."

"But we don't know for sure that they'll come back," Aris said and then looked past him to one of the shelves. "Rituals in Death," it read. She dropped her gaze. *Even when you think you're going to die, you never actually think you're going to die.* Was this the same stubbornness that got her mother killed?

Yuki shook his head. "My mother will not be taking that chance, especially now that her thesis has been stolen as well."

Alek crouched down, collecting the scattered bills. He turned and said, "You really think they're connected?"

"You heard what he said about the guards," Yuki said. "Sounds like magic to me." Alek paused with a handful of bills. He stared at the ground a moment before reaching for the next bill. Aris knelt to help him and Yuki reached out to grab her arm. "If I were you, I'd think about telling your parents the truth, and then getting the hell out of here." He dropped his hand. "As far as I'm concerned, either we find Krysidia, or we find a new city to live in."

Aris stretched for a fifty-dollar bill caught under one of the table legs. So she'd either lose her family or her friends. Some choice that was. "There has to be a third option," Aris said, her voice thick.

"There is." Yuki shrugged. "Death."

She probably should have seen that one coming. Yuki was right—she really was a sad excuse for a prophet. And now, if they didn't find Krysidia, she'd lose all hope of improving. Aris handed Alek a pile of bills, slightly astounded by the amount of cash he so casually carried around. But then again, it wasn't like anyone could rob him. She dragged herself back into her chair and buried her head in her arms. When they first told her about Anathemians who couldn't use magic, Krysidia had just been a word. But now that she knew about ley lines and meridians, it felt . . . different. "Even if we manage to find Krysidia," she said, lifting her chin, "how do we know it'll be any better?"

Yuki wrapped his arms around his sides, hugging himself as he shrugged. "Because it has to be." His voice broke as he spoke.

She knew getting lured to that shop hadn't exactly been her fault. Even so, Lochlen had only brought them there to see if they could contact her parents. And at this rate, Yuki and Mirai would soon be halfway across the country and the rest of them would likely follow. She thought about her trip to the mountains with Alek—about the strange feeling in her stomach and the familiarly crooked tree. It was probably nothing, but still . . . Aris bit her lip. If she was going to lose them anyway, then . . . She turned to Yuki. "Have you ever read anything about contorted trees?"

His head tilted, eyebrows dipping. She expected him to snub her suggestion, but he eagerly disappeared into the shelves again. Several books thudded to the floor and Yuki raced back to the table. He slammed something down, his face wide with interest.

Alek's eyes darted to a small red book with gold foiling. "I've never seen that before."

Yuki looked up. "Neither have I. It was jutting out at the end of Taoism. I don't know how I didn't notice it sooner."

Alek and Aris craned over him as he flipped to the first page. "Taoism?" Alek said, moving to get a closer look at the text. "But that doesn't make any sense. Isn't this Welsh?"

"Welsh poetry, actually."

Aris leaned forward. "How can you tell?"

"I can read upward of thirty languages," Yuki said, as if it wasn't a big deal. Aris remembered Mirai saying he was a genius, but that was just wild.

"Well, now I feel extremely unaccomplished." She scratched the side of her neck.

"Don't." Alek nudged her shoulder. "If he wasn't wearing that bracelet, he'd be stuck using Google Translate with the rest of us."

Aris bit her lip. "How does it work?"

"The same way as Mirai's," Yuki said, "except where her physical abilities are heightened, my mental processes are amplified."

It was almost unfair; Aris's powers just left her haunted with the memory of her mother's dying breath. Meanwhile, Yuki could probably read *The Odyssey* in its original Greek. She picked through the strands of her hair. "I don't suppose you'd ever want to trade crystals for a weekend?" she mused.

"What?" Yuki flicked his gaze upward. "You would trade powers with someone like me?" He cocked his head. "Did you hear that, Alek? A prophet is jealous of my powers." His grin was mocking. "You don't even know how rare you are, do you?" *Rare.* "Not that it works like that anyway. Our powers are hereditary. As far as I can tell, our crystals are interchangeable. And as much as I'd love to test that theory further, I'm not willing to risk my own powers for curiosity's sake." Yuki slapped a hand down on the table. "Now, if you're done fawning over my talents, I'd like to get back to reading what is possibly the most intriguing bit of information I've come across since middle school."

Aris bit back a smile, trying not to let the word *rare* go straight to her head. She turned back to the book and the boy flipping furiously through its pages. "What's so exciting about Welsh poetry anyway? I mean, besides the obvious."

Yuki waved her off. "I'm tired of explaining things."

Alek took a deep breath and said, "How much do you know about Celtic mythology?"

She bobbed her head. "More than most teenagers, I suspect."

"Have you heard of Tuatha Dé Danann?" Alek continued, playing with one of the buttons on his jacket. "The race of supernatural—"

"Faeries," Aris finished.

His eyes brightened. "You know it then?"

"I've read the legend."

"So you know that they're believed to be the first inhabitants of Ireland, said to have lived there for several years until they were chased out. That they disappeared under the foothills . . ."

"Alek." Aris batted her lashes. "Are you saying I'm a faerie?"

He shrugged. "I'm saying we've been called by many names. *Faeries* just happens to be one of the nicer ones."

Yuki was mumbling something about a waxing moon that regressed when there was a knock on the door. Then a second, and a third. He paused.

"Shit," Alek said.

Yuki shoved the book in his bag and shooed Aris toward the door. The three of them brushed past the guard on their way out, leaving nothing behind except a single brown bill fluttering to the ground.

CHAPTER 22

Faeries didn't have wings, not originally, and even as Aris shaded them in, she felt a bit silly. But wings were fun to draw, and her hands needed the distraction. She dragged her pencil, lengthening the ends of Mirai's thick hair. The first sketch had been an accident. It wasn't until she'd finished detailing the faerie prince's hair that she realized she'd drawn Alek. As soon as she dropped her hand, it became embarrassingly obvious. She'd drawn his heavy, slanted brows; the soft curve of his lip; and the dimple that appeared only on his left cheek, never his right, which, as far as she could tell, was the only asymmetrical thing about him.

As fourth period ended, Aris flipped through her collection. Besides Alek, she'd done Yuki, Jada, and Mirai, each with their own set of wings and pointed ears to match. She turned to a fresh page, realizing there was only one faerie left to draw—

The bell sounded and she stretched out her fingers before tucking her sketchbook into the depths of her bag.

When she got to her locker, she dug her arm into a pile of books and pulled out a sandwich that looked as though a car had hit it. In fact, the entire shelf looked like a car had hit it. Beneath the weight of textbooks she usually lugged back and forth, the metal was warping. But between the ghost stories and the mythologies, she barely had time to breathe. Alek had sent her so many articles that she was starting to feel like a fraud for ever considering herself a nerd. With a sigh, she traded the contents of her bag for the misshapen cucumber sandwich and dragged her feet to the lunchroom.

Haley and Jamie had already snagged a table, and Aris hesitated a moment before joining them. Of course, then she remembered that choosing to sit alone would have been the high school equivalent of throwing down her gauntlet, and so with a deep breath, she sauntered over and took up the seat across from Haley.

"Where's Devon?" Aris asked to break the ice.

"No idea," Haley said. "She and Taisha ditched again."

Aris let out a small, polite laugh—a period at the end of a sentence.

Jamie, too, was less chatty than usual. He and Aris quietly ate their lunches while Haley talked about their plans for next year. In the meantime, Alek had texted at least half a dozen new links, and when Aris finished her sandwich, she thumbed through and picked the last one. Her screen jumped to a wall of text and despite how long she scrolled, she could never seem to reach the end. Aris slumped forward.

At least now she knew what she was looking for—sort of. Yuki said if they could figure out the direction of the ley line, it should lead them to the portal. But it was one of those things that sounded a lot easier in theory. And it didn't help that the ruins—the one point they knew intersected with the ley line—were invisible. With an elbow propped up on the table, Aris leaned her head against her hand and started reading.

As much as she wanted to help them find Krysidia, she couldn't help but feel as though her efforts were futile. It was like giving a first grader ten years' worth of math homework and then expecting them to win the Fields Medal. And maybe that would've been easy for someone like Yuki, but to Aris it seemed impossible.

As she attempted to focus on the article, her cheek slid all the way down her hand until her breath threatened to fog up her phone screen. She dug her fingers into her hair, thinking about the decrepit tree she'd seen in the mountains and how she was going to end up looking just like it if she kept staying up all night. But the more she thought about the tree, the more she felt as if she'd seen it before. A part of her wanted to suggest they go back. That they ask Lochlen to tag along and see if he recognized anything. But time was now of the essence, and they couldn't afford to go gallivanting through the mountains on a whim. At least, not anymore. Would Alek leave too? Where he would go if he did? Could she go with him? Would he want her to?

Aris still hadn't decided whether to tell her parents. Honestly, she was waiting to talk to Mirai about it, but since that day at the shop, Mirai had been spending all her time at the dojo, no doubt swinging around that katana—

"Aris." Haley waved a hand in front of her screen. "I asked you a question."

"Sorry," Aris said, without looking up. She was wondering if all this time getting up to speed on ley lines would be better spent training with Mirai.

Haley huffed and then, when Aris still didn't raise her head, made a point of clicking her heels beneath the table. "You know, I never thought you'd turn out to be *that* girl," she said bitterly. "The kind that ditches all her friends the second she gets a boyfriend."

Aris frowned. "I don't think he's my boyfriend." *Unless . . .* Did Alek consider himself her boyfriend? It wasn't as if he'd ever said the word out loud, but he had been acting quite boyfriend-ish lately, with picking her up and dropping her off. Although that had more to do with the shopkeeper than any sort of romantic notion. Watching the lightning storm could kind of be considered a date. But on the other hand—

"Aris!"

"What?" she said back, with a bit too much force.

Haley blinked as if she'd just been insulted. "What, now you're too cool to talk to me?" She crossed her arms. "I think you're letting all this attention get to your head." Aris's mind went straight to Alek again, realizing Haley was probably right. Alek was just trying to look out for her as a *friend*. "Believe me, I get it," Haley continued. "I mean, I saw his car. I. Get. It. But everyone thinks you dumped Brent for some super wealthy private school boy. Aren't you worried that makes you sound like a snob?"

Aris scrolled through Alek's message, hoping all the links he'd sent weren't as long as the first. "I don't think it's a private school," she said, suddenly imagining them all in uniforms.

"Whatever, okay. My point is you brought him to class with you, and now Brent has to deal with all these rumors swirling around. Don't you think that's a bit unfair?"

Aris lifted her chin. "And who was it that started all those rumors in the first place?"

Haley withdrew. "There were at least fifty people at that party. It could've been anyone." She turned to Jamie, whose neck had been equally craned over his phone this entire time. "Brent doesn't start stuff like that, right? I mean, obviously you wouldn't be friends with someone like that."

When Jamie raised his head, his eyes locked in on Aris. "Aren't girls supposed to stick together and all that?" he said, turning to face Haley. "It's not like Aris has any control over what people say about her."

"Well, yeah, like, I know." Haley ran a hand through her hair. "That's why I'm telling her this. I'm literally trying to help her. But it's kinda hard when she's had her eyes glued to her phone this entire time."

Jamie took a deep breath and pushed out his chest in a stretch. "Whatever." He went back to staring at his phone, but not before glancing Aris over, the hint of a smile on his lips. Aris had expected the underhanded snark he usually shot her way; this was something different. This smile was softer, the kind that could make someone blush. But instead of turning pink, Aris's cheeks lost their color entirely. Her face grayed as she recoiled. This was the boy who'd *despised* her for the better half of a year.

Aris's chest burned with someone else's jealousy, and she turned to see Haley's lips wobble. Her eyes bounced from table to table, but her fingers were curled into fists. Aris's stomach flipped, but this time she was pretty sure it was her own sense of dread, rather than Haley's resentment. But then again, it could've been suspicion. Or maybe the feeling was coming from Jamie? Maybe it was embarrassment? But that wouldn't make much sense. She touched a finger to her forehead. Everything muddled together as if her powers were fighting against her. The more she tried to figure out what Haley was feeling, the louder her head became.

Aris desperately needed some fresh air. She wanted to pull Haley outside and reassure her that nothing was going on between her and Jamie, but defending herself seemingly out of nowhere would probably just make her look guilty. Aris remembered the last time Haley had been upset with Jamie. Aris had asked her about it, and Haley denied the feeling altogether. Of course, that was before Aris met Alek, and so she'd tried to tell Haley how obvious it was, but Haley just accused her of projecting. At the time, she thought it was her way of saying she didn't want to talk about it, but now, Aris knew better than to bring up Haley's jealousy. She was the only one besides Haley who'd felt it, and mentioning it would do more harm than good.

Aris bit her lip, realizing the irony of her powers—they could so easily be used for evil. A lump settled in the pit of her stomach as she remembered the definition she'd stumbled across after foolishly searching the word *Anathemian*: an accursed thing; something monstrous or evil. And then, as if on cue, somebody took up the seat beside her.

Brent.

Aris wrapped her arms around her sides, wishing desperately to disappear. He'd been avoiding her until now, or maybe Aris had just been better at avoiding him. "I saw you in the parking lot the other morning," Brent said. "You were getting dropped off by that Adam guy, right?"

Aris took a steadying breath. "His name's Alek."

"Right, Alek." Brent dragged out the name as if trying to carve it into his memory. Although Aris suspected it was already ingrained there, especially considering what Brent said next. "So are you two shacking up or what?"

"Wait, you slept with him?" Haley exclaimed.

Brent shot Aris a wolfish grin. "He seems pretty loaded too. I'll admit, I never had you pegged as a gold digger."

In that moment, Aris wished Alek's powers hadn't been so kind. The word *monstrous* came to mind again, and she regretted the thought. So instead, she wished Mirai was here. Or Alek. Hell, at this point she would've settled for Lochlen. She just wanted someone on her side. Her stomach clenched as she remembered Mirai might not be around much longer.

Aris's mind drifted to her parents again before ending up on her mother. Was she here? Was she lingering in the corner, wishing her daughter was strong enough to stand up for herself?

Aris wanted to be. She wanted to be strong. She needed to be able to defend herself, and she needed to do it without anyone else's help. She glanced to the back wall, where she pictured her mother's spirit giving her a nod of encouragement, and then she shot up from the table. "You know what—" Her eyes cut to Brent, and she could've sworn she saw him flinch. But then she realized how loud her words had been. A few heads had turned in her direction. Haley, Jamie, and Brent were all staring directly at her.

Then came the smoke, thick black clouds of it. But this time, the flames burned cold. She felt a dozen icy stares from around the room. Or maybe they were fingers. Yes. A dozen icy fingers clawing at her back. It was the dead of winter, and the air was so cold it choked her very breath. Aris looked down at her trembling hands, realizing they were bare. Her gauntlet had been thrown down and everyone at the table was waiting to hear her challenge. Sheepishly, Aris wondered if it was too late to bend over and pick it back up, because a tiny voice was screaming *run* in one ear and *hide* in the other. But Aris was frozen solid. She was encased in a thin sheet of ice, and she knew that the moment she moved, time would follow. She'd be forced to finish her sentence with words she'd either lost or had never actually thought of.

A phone buzzed, and the table vibrated with it. Aris's shell began to crack and when she looked down, she could've cried. It was *her* phone rattling against the table. She scrambled for the device and fled the cafeteria without a word, but as she bounded around the corner, she noticed the name lit up across her screen. Hesitantly, she accepted the call. "What is it?"

"Well, hello to you too," Lochlen said.

Aris let out a breath. "Why are you calling me?" She pushed through a set of doors and let the fresh air hit her.

"Maybe I just missed that delightful temper of yours."

"In that case—"

"Don't hang up," Lochlen interjected, and Aris dragged the phone back up to her ear.

The two of them sat in silence for a minute, wind crackling through the microphone on his end. "Listen, my lunch hour's almost over so . . ."

"Did something happen?" Lochlen asked. His voice was different this time, but Aris couldn't quite place the change. It wasn't any higher or lower, just different. "I mean, is everything okay?"

Her stomach suddenly felt empty again. Aris took a seat on the step and wrapped her arm around the railing. "Yeah," she breathed. "Everything's fine." At least now it was. She thought about her near self-destruction a minute ago. Could Lochlen have known? She scanned the parking lot, part of her expecting to find the gloomy boy off in the distance. When she didn't, Aris looked for anyone else who might be watching. Not only was she out in the open, but she was completely alone—basically the two things Alek had warned her to avoid. "Is that it then?" The breeze caught Aris's hair, and she brushed it out of her face, tucking a piece behind her ear to secure it.

"No," Lochlen blurted. "Actually, I was wondering if you had any plans today." His words sort of trailed off and Aris pictured him tracing circles on the ground with his finger. "Alek didn't mention anything, so I figured you were free."

She frowned. "Because the only plans I could possibly have would involve Alek?"

"You do have plans, then?" Lochlen said, and Aris couldn't shake the disappointment in his voice.

"Well, no, but—"

"Great. I'll pick you up after school."

"Wait, what?"

"Shit." Aris heard a clambering as Lochlen mumbled, "I have to go," and then he hung up.

Aris thought about heading back inside to look for Haley, but as she sat on the concrete steps, with the familiar feeling of grit beneath her hands, she remembered the way Alek and Lochlen had fought outside the shop and the chaos that could've ensued. She and Haley had never fought that fiercely. Aris used to think it was a good thing, that it meant they got along, but now she suspected it was because neither of them really cared that much about the other. Lochlen and Alek had looked like fire and gasoline and yet, after all that, Alek had put a hand on Lochlen's shoulder. Maybe fighting was part of what brought them closer. The way heating and cooling a piece of steel forged a stronger sword.

Aris was still outside when the first bell rang. She dragged herself up off the stairs and headed back to her locker. She was turning a corner when someone ran into her. Books scattered across the hallway. Aris quickly bent over to help pick them up. When she looked up, Garret was crouched down beside her, flustered. He went to grab the same book she reached for and accidentally touched her hand. Garret dropped the last of the books still tucked under his arm.

One of his textbooks fell open to reveal a drawing skillfully shaded on the back of one of his old quizzes. A detailed image of a human heart stared up at her. Literally stared. In the center of the heart was an eye that looked as though it were struggling to stay open. But it was the hand near the top of the page that intrigued her the most. Four chains hung down like marionette strings, each controlling a different chamber. Aris picked it up. "You drew this?"

Garret nodded shyly. "Just something to occupy my hand."

Aris handed it back to him. She'd almost forgotten how much they had in common. After her parents' accident, she'd been forced to change schools; Garret was the only one who wasn't afraid to sit with her when everyone else thought being an orphan meant she had a highly contagious disease.

Looking at him now, he seemed pretty much the same. Maybe a tad longer, like someone had taken the seven-year-old and stretched him out a bit. He still had a deep set of brown eyes and a smattering of freckles across his nose and cheeks, barely visible against his dark skin.

She eyed the sketchbook on the ground. "Is there more? Can I see?" She reached out an arm, but Garret slapped a hand over the book.

"Sorry," he mumbled. "It's just . . . they're a bit private."

Aris shook her head. "It's okay, I shouldn't have asked." They may have been close once, but that was a long time ago. They were little more than strangers now, and Aris knew better than anyone how vulnerable it was to share your drawings with someone. For a moment, she considered how her life might have turned out if the two of them had stayed friends after elementary school.

Garret returned to his feet, but still looked off balance. His face was flushed and Aris was worried he might be ill. She was just about to ask if he wanted her to walk him to the nurse when Mr. Matthews stepped out of his classroom.

"The bell's going to ring any second now. Go on, get to class," he said into the hallway. When the teacher glanced in their direction, Garret gathered up the rest of his books and darted past her down the hall. Aris felt a brush of wind as she stood back up.

She continued down the hall, hoping Garret wasn't as sick as he seemed, but when she opened her locker, Aris felt just as shaky as Garret had looked. Her stomach twisted as she stared at her rearranged belongings in disbelief. She reached for a textbook that was neatly stacked with several others, spines all facing outwards in perfect unison.

CHAPTER 23

"You're taking me antiquing?" Aris asked, leaning against the side of a Volkswagen, staring up at a building that was twice as tall as it was wide. Tarnished window frames convened in pairs between ruddy bricks—as though the shop itself had been sliced off the end of an old apartment complex, and the double set of doors stationed on the far left were painted an awful sort of red that reminded Aris of dried blood.

Lochlen twirled a set of keys around his finger. "Not exactly."

Aris wrinkled her brow. She rapped the hood of the Volkswagen with a loosely curled fist, eyeing the only other car in the lot. It's not as if she wanted to believe Lochlen would take her somewhere dangerous, but at the same time, he'd waited to tell them about the second presence at The Twisted Juniper, and he'd lied about the license plate.

He slipped the keys into the pocket of his faded black hoodie. "I thought you wanted me to teach you something useful."

A third car pulled into a spot two rows down, and Aris glanced over at the elderly gentleman behind the wheel.

The place wasn't exactly bustling with witnesses, but then again, it's not as if she was going in alone. Lochlen would be with her, and honestly, she might not have too many chances left to learn from him.

The inside of the shop was a labyrinth of desks and antique dressers, each cluttered with vintage cannisters, lampshades, and rotary dial phones. Every wall was covered with foggy mirrors and heavy picture frames, making Aris feel as though she'd just walked into a carnival funhouse. She stared at her feet to keep from tripping as Lochlen guided her to the back of the room, but as Aris brushed past a headless doll, she began to get a bad feeling about accepting Lochlen's offer.

He stopped near a set of encyclopedias, eyes darting over the rest of the shop. He flicked the side of a globe, watching it spin. "The reason you could see your parents' accident is that objects can sometimes absorb the surrounding energy." He stopped the globe, his finger landing somewhere in the northern Atlantic Ocean. "Most memories won't be as vivid as that one, but you should at least be able to identify a feeling."

Aris leaned a hand against a giant birdcage. "Wouldn't it be easier to start with people?" she asked as a thick layer of dust transferred like grill marks onto her skin. "You know"—she frowned at her palm—"while their emotions are still fresh?" She wiped her hand down the front of her jeans.

"No."

Aris pursed her lips. "Despite what you may think, I'm not entirely incompetent. I'm actually pretty good at reading emotions," she said matter-of-factly. And then, after flicking open a music box that didn't produce any sound, her voice dwindled. "I just didn't realize I was the only one who could."

"That woman over there," Lochlen said, nodding to a girl who'd walked in and darted to a display of letter openers. "What is she feeling?"

Aris pressed her tongue to her cheek and said, "Like she's gotten a lot of mail lately?"

Lochlen rolled his eyes. "I don't doubt you can sense feelings, especially intense ones, but if that ability is going to be of any use to you, then you'll need to learn how to distinguish emotions." He gave the woman another glance before disappearing behind a large folding desk. Aris darted after him, down a hallway she hadn't known was there. She weaved between floor lamps and empty scotch bottles as Lochlen continued. "The problem with people is that they're impulsive. By the time you think you've figured them out, their emotions have already shifted. But something like this, for example"—Lochlen scooped up a matchbox—"is likely to have a single, dormant feeling. Usually the last memory, or the most frequent." He slid the metal lid back and forth. "With enough practice, you'll start to notice similarities between objects. If you can discern those similarities, you can group them, and once you assign a word to that feeling, well, it's really no different from memorizing a deck of tarot cards." They turned a corner, entering a room where dozens of chandeliers hung from the rafters. Lochlen stooped a little, discarding the matchbox on a nearby shelf. "Come back and find me when you've gotten the hang of it."

As Lochlen turned to leave, Aris grabbed the hem of his hoodie. "Wait," she breathed, and Lochlen went incredulously still. Her pulse quickened as she looked down to where her fingers clung to faded black fabric. It was ironic, all that notion of wanting to be strong, wanting to be able to defend herself, and here she was, nearly begging Lochlen not to leave her side. Aris dropped her hand. "Never mind," she murmured, and slunk off to a row of armoires.

She opened a drawer full of jumbled necklaces that reminded her of her locker, or at least, how she'd left it before lunch. She hadn't realized that being afraid wasn't the same as feeling unsafe, but now she imagined it was the difference between walking home at night with a phone pressed to her ear, and actually being followed. Learning that her mother's ring had made her a target was like walking around with her phone pressed to her ear, but opening her locker this afternoon and finding her textbooks neatly stacked . . . that was like crossing the street and noticing a figure cross it behind you.

Safety was something Aris took for granted. In fact, it was something so natural to her that even now, even after her parents and Mirai's aunt, after the threat at the shop and the break-in at the library, her mind was still struggling to grasp the gravity of the situation.

Expecting danger was different from being faced with it, and Aris was lost in transition. Her security blanket hadn't been ripped off her shoulders; it'd been slowly shredded with a dulled blade. A hole here. A rip there. *Nothing to worry about*, she'd thought. *Still wearable*, she'd reckoned. And now, Aris clung to the scraps and pretended they were a shield. She gripped them as tightly as she'd clung to Lochlen's sweater.

With one hand tucked into her sleeve, she sifted through a lump of chains. What if Lochlen had been at her school today? She thought about his freshly pressed clothes and how meticulously her locker had been rearranged. It would make sense for him to have been there. How else could he have known what happened in the cafeteria?

She picked up a pendent and a second necklace dangled from where the two chains knotted together. Lochlen hadn't been wrong about her inability to distinguish emotions. Aris thought about the way Haley's feelings seemed to glob together with Jamie's and her own. She dropped the pair of necklaces and shut the drawer. A can of buttons toppled over as the armoire swayed, and Aris remembered the clamber she'd heard right before Lochlen ended their call. It could've been the sound of a locker door. It could've been *her* locker door.

When Aris slid open the second drawer, she found a bracelet strewn among a bed of teaspoons. On a chain of dark iron, tiny copper suns alternated with gold stars and silver crescents. She slouched forward, smiling down at the suns smug little faces, but then she noticed the tag and straightened. The stars must've been plated with actual gold, and it was amazing the thing ended up tossed in a drawer. At that price, you'd think they'd have kept it behind a case of glass.

She looped a finger through the chain, wondering what emotion had been burned into the iron, but the sun felt cold as she touched it. Her finger was skimming the curve of one moon when she heard a soft exhale. Aris whirled, reaching for whatever was close enough to grab.

Next thing she knew, she was staring up at Lochlen with her knees slightly bent and a brass candlestick holder pointed at one of his eyes. He looked startled, but not in the way she would've expected. Instead, his gaze dropped from the brass taper to Aris's eyes, his lips slightly parted as his chest fell. She could feel his question and how badly he wanted to ask it, and she could feel the answer. But that was it. There were no words. It was like trying to read a foreign language. Aris took a step back, lowering the candlestick holder slightly. Her heel knocked a stack of film cannisters and the sound of skittering metal distracted them both. Aris set the taper down beside a fireplace poker, perplexed as to why she hadn't grabbed that instead.

Lochlen dipped his chin. "You're worried about the shopkeeper." It was more of a statement than a question, but Aris gave a slight nod. Lochlen was quiet for a long time, then said, "I'm sorry . . . about your mother." His voice was swollen.

She fiddled with a broach she found on one of the tables, careful not to prick her finger. "Actually, I've been meaning to thank you." He stiffened a little, and Aris set the broach back down. "I know the visit didn't exactly go as planned, but I don't think I would have recognized her if you hadn't taught me how to read a photo." The hint of a smile tugged at her lips. "And while I may not have actually talked to her or anything, I got this feeling, like maybe I'm the reason she hung around this long. That there's something she wanted me to know, or—I don't know. I'm probably reading too much into it. I just—I can't help but think she'll find me again."

Lochlen suddenly looked ashen, and Aris's smile vanished. His fingers found the edge of a tapestry and his eyes found the ground. "I don't know if Alek mentioned this," he said, "but my grandmother wasn't a prophet like us. She was a reaper." A string came loose from the corner of the tapestry and Lochlen tugged at it further. "What happened to your mom—what she did, well, there's no coming back from that." He dropped his hands, prying his eyes from the floor and seeming to force himself to look at her. "You won't see her again. I'm sorry."

Aris cupped a hand over her mouth, but it was less from grief than shock. Until now, she'd assumed they were being overcautious. She thought the notion that the shopkeeper had set them up was a worst-case scenario, that the second presence could've been a coincidence rather than a threat. But now she understood why everyone else was so tense. For twelve years, her mother had clung to—as the shopkeeper would say—a life that no longer served her. *Twelve years.* Whatever threat Lochlen sensed had been real. Real enough for her mother to sacrifice her connection to this world—to Aris.

The elderly gentleman she recognized from the parking lot wandered in from down the hallway and Lochlen took a half step in front of her. "Come with me," he whispered, before winding back through the shop and guiding her up a staircase.

They passed the second floor, continuing straight to the third. The steps creaked loudly beneath their feet, probably alerting the entire shop of their whereabouts. Of course, the elderly gentleman wasn't actually a threat, and Lochlen wasn't really ushering her to safety; he just hadn't wanted to be overheard talking about ghosts.

The third floor was a large single room separated into aisles, but it had an elegance about it that the main level lacked. Lace fabrics hung down in one corner, and cases full of china crowded the other.

"Nobody else is up here, so you're free to practice as ridiculously as you'd like," Lochlen said, his voice slack, as if he hadn't just told her that her mother had basically died all over again. "Try to find metal objects if you can."

"Why metal?" Aris turned around, but Lochlen was already gone.

She didn't know why she'd expected him to stay. Why, when he'd told her to follow him, Aris had assumed it was because he cared about her wellbeing. Lochlen wasn't Alek. His priority wasn't to protect her. It was to teach her, and he'd done his part. Now, the rest was up to her.

As she crept through trinket-packed shelves, Aris hoped one of the objects would jump out at her. The first few items she picked up had felt cold—empty, just as the bracelet had. She rounded a corner.

The gasp that came out of Aris's mouth would've been embarrassing if she hadn't been alone, and for the first time, she found herself relieved that Lochlen had abandoned her. She darted across the aisle to a Sailor Moon music clock, half hidden behind a baby-blue teapot. It was faded, and the sailor's skirt had a few scuffs, but Aris knew one thing for certain: Evie would *love* it. She weaved a hand around the porcelain spout and plucked it from the shelf. She was looking for the price tag when she noticed a pocket watch that must've been tucked between the clock and the teapot.

Before even touching it, Aris knew it had a memory. She stashed the Sailor Moon clock in a nearby cabinet and wrapped the long bronze chain around her thumb. With the pocket watch warming in her hand, Aris tried to remember what Lochlen had said about reading a photo.

She closed her eyes, only to open them. She tried again, this time alongside a breath, but something brushed her elbow and she nearly took down a coat rack as she leaped sideways. There was a difference between being afraid and feeling unsafe, and right now, Aris was afraid.

Lochlen had said she was alone, and she would've heard the floorboards creak if anyone else had ventured up here, though neither of those facts could stop her heart from racing. And once again, Aris found herself wishing for Lochlen or Alek or Mirai, for another pair of eyes to stand guard while hers were shut. She shook off the thought. She wanted to be stronger, *needed* to be stronger.

Instead of relying on another pair of eyes, she convinced herself to trust her ears, forced herself to believe no one could sneak up on her. And then, with another shaky breath and a pocket watch clutched between her fingers, she shoved her fears to the side.

This time, when Aris closed her eyes, they stayed closed. *This time*, instead of focusing on what she couldn't see, she focused on what she could. Aris pictured the pocket watch with as much detail as possible: the case, a slightly darker bronze than the chain, was embossed with delicate swirls of leaves. She clicked it open in her mind's eye and the clock face appeared. The hands weren't accurate, not even close, but in an effort to avoid distraction, she focused on the color. Not the color of the watch, but the color behind it. The color that had once made the lifeless hands tick.

And just like that, the watch in her head began to ooze. The fluid was all-consuming, a slow gray essence that seemed to drag everything down. It reminded her of a Salvador Dali painting—the one with the melting clocks. *The Persistence of Memory* he'd called it.

But just like the painting, the image seemed almost impossible to describe with words. She could think of a hundred: guilt, anger, loneliness.

But none of them were quite right because despite how heavy it felt in her hand, the watch was laced with happy memories too. They lingered in the background, like a sun peeking over the horizon. Although the thought of them made her stomach flip.

Her eyes shot open and her back stiffened; she'd been so lost in the memory that she'd stopped listening for the floorboards. She waited for a creak, or a breath, and then, when she was certain she was still alone, Aris unfurled her hand. Grief. That was the word she chose. And it made discarding the watch feel somewhat disrespectful. Instead of hiding it back behind the teapot, Aris propped it against a glass bottle on one of the higher shelves. Then she selected a new corridor to explore, her hands stretched straight out as she walked.

The model ship that brushed her fingers was more wood than metal, but she tried it anyway. Repeating the same steps as before, Aris closed her eyes. She pictured masts stiffened to look like wind was permanently blowing and the delicate cords fastening them down. This time, the energy she saw was bright. It launched itself out from behind the boat like fireworks in a brilliant array of crimson and orange. This feeling was a child holding a stick as if it were a sword. It was a child who climbed hills as if they were mountains, who leaped over canyons in the form of sidewalk cracks. *This* was a child who constructed a ship as if they were the engineer, the captain, and the stowaway all rolled into one.

As she opened her eyes, the surrounding shelves were no longer packed with trinkets, they were brimming with treasure. Aris threw a hand over her mouth to muffle the laugh that bubbled up from her throat. Was this what Lochlen meant when he told her to practice as ridiculously as she wanted?

Even as the feeling faded, Aris was left with a sense of awe. Because although she was no longer surrounded by piles of treasure, and she had neither a stick nor a sword, Aris had something most children could only ever dream of. Magic.

As her hands danced across the windows of a cabinet, she wondered why it had seemed perfectly normal to read a person's feelings, and yet she'd never once thought to try an object. She twirled a finger along the rim of a silver goblet and a puff of dark purple smoke drifted upward. It gathered into a cloud loosely resembling a skull and then dissipated. Resentment, Aris decided as she moved on to a pair of reading glasses. There was a tightness in the eyes, like the dainty frames were hindering vision instead of aiding it. Aris smacked her lips together, wanting to rinse the bitterness from her mouth.

As she looped around to the next aisle, Aris touched a brooding belt buckle, an envious pair of earrings, and an agitated ashtray, before pressing up on her toes to reach a rusted flask. Whoever its previous owner was had been, in a word, *dizzy*. She drew her arm back, stumbling against the side of a desk. Her hand landed hard on its surface, fingers grazing the silver handle of a hairbrush.

The hairbrush struck her like a bolt of electricity, pain forcing her eyes shut. She tried to open them, but a vision sank icy claws into her skin, begging to be heard.

Aris watched the hairbrush clatter to the floor as a young girl was yanked from her chair. It all happened so fast. A man pulled out a gun. A woman dropped to the ground. The girl who'd been yanked from her chair was crying as the barrel of a pistol pressed against her skull. The woman started screaming, long breathless sobs, as useless as stones hurled at an oncoming train. Aris winced as the man brought a hand to the child, but the woman lunged forward before he could strike.

Aris couldn't tell what happened next. Her ears were ringing. The man was gone. The gun was on the floor and . . . the floor was covered in blood, more than she ever thought possible. It welled out from beneath the young girl, who lay unmoving, and Aris sucked in a breath, trying to clear the metallic scent from her nose.

Aris didn't realize she was on the ground until she blinked and found Lochlen kneeling in front of her. Her ears were ringing with the echoes of a sob, and for a moment all she could see were his eyes: heavily dilated, intensely focused, eyes that held on to their own breath. Eyes darting frantically, searching for a button to press, something to end her suffering. There was a hand on her cheek. Fingers half buried in her hair. So close to the nape of her neck . . . And then he was helping her up.

With his hand holding hers, Lochlen guided her down the staircase, but he moved slowly, as if worried she'd forgotten how to walk. And maybe she had. She couldn't feel her legs moving, but every time she looked back, the number of steps behind them had grown.

Everything on the first floor looked threatening. The chandeliers tried to grab her as they walked by, empty cannisters oozed, clock hands spun uncontrollably. Even the empty picture frames swayed, crying out to her as they rocked.

Out. She had to get out.

"I know," Lochlen said, but his voice was muffled, as if underwater.

When she glanced down, he was still holding her hand. It was the same hand that wore her ring and as the amethyst sparkled against his pale skin, Aris felt as if she was remembering something. A memory was knocking, only she couldn't find the door to let it in. She kept turning around, checking each wall, looking for a handle or a knob. But there were dozens of them, piles of doorhandles in every shape, size, and color. They were spread out across one of the tables and as Aris veered for them, a hand gently tugged her back.

It was in front of her now. The door. But the knocking had stopped, replaced once again by the dreaded ring of muffled sobs. This door was not the one she'd been looking for. *This door* was an awful sort of red. The color of dried blood.

And then Aris was sitting in the car again with Lochlen leaning over her lap as he dug through the glove compartment. When he pulled out a tiny vial and touched a thumb to either side of her temple, all she could think about was the hand holding her cheek steady. As he pulled back, her nose filled with the scent of lemongrass, and it flushed out the metallic tang left on her tongue. The car was already started, its grumbling bubbling into her ears. Aris stared at the fuel gauge, focusing on the thin dial until she could see with perfect clarity just how little gas the Volkswagen had. "What did you do?" Aris asked, blinking.

Lochlen returned the vial to the glove compartment. "It's not anything weird, just some essential oils." He looked her over as if counting each piece, making sure he hadn't left any part of her behind. "My mom mixed this one just in case I . . . well, just in case. It's meant to clear your head." She nodded, but her gaze was once again fixed on the door, on the color she couldn't get out of her head. "Aris, I'm sorr—"

"Can we go somewhere else?" she asked, clawing for her seatbelt.

Lochlen didn't press her. He simply flicked the radio to the station he'd complained about on the way to the ruins and took off down the road.

CHAPTER 24

A ris picked at her nails. They'd only been driving for ten minutes, but the silence made it feel like an hour. She was curled over on herself, her face pressed against the window when Lochlen said, "Close your eyes."

"What?"

"Close your eyes and hold out your hand," he insisted as he dug into his pocket.

Aris scowled. "Um, no?"

Lochlen kept his fist tightly locked. "Oh just shut up and do it."

Aris made a big deal of following his directions, and when something cold dropped into her palm, a chill traveled up her arm and all the way back down her spine until her whole body tingled. The bracelet in front of her was a mix of tiny suns and stars and moons. Aris stilled, a question in her mind instead of on her tongue.

"Do you like it?" Lochlen prodded, but Aris didn't respond. Instead, she stared down at the bracelet, waiting, as if the smug little faces would eventually answer for her. "I really hadn't planned to leave you for as long as I did," he admitted, his voice dipping, "but there was this tiny old lady with eyes like a bloody hawk and *I swear*, I must've circled that shop a dozen times before managing to shake her."

Eyes like a hawk? "Wait, did you steal this?" Aris snapped. He shrugged. "Lochlen!"

"What?"

"We have to take it back."

"No one will even notice it's gone," he drawled, slowing down instead of speeding up as the light in front of them turned amber. Aris sank back in her seat, telling herself that arguing with Lochlen was futile. But maybe a small part of her didn't want to take the bracelet back, not really.

Aris turned back to the window, pretending to be repulsed by his disregard for the law. She had expected Lochlen to take her home, but he'd brought them somewhere downtown. They wandered along the sidewalk, stopping in front of a tearoom. Aris grinned cheekily. "Let me guess, you're going to teach me to read tea leaves?"

Lochlen gave her a look. "No," he said dismissively.

Frowning, she followed him inside. "So, why did you bring me here?" she said with a sigh.

He shook his head. "Does everything always have to be about you?" Aris's face warmed as Lochlen selected a table by the window. "Isn't it obvious?" he said. "I wanted some tea."

A server came by to take their orders and deliver an assortment of fixings: various sugars and honey, a small jug of milk, and a selection of empty cups. Aris looked at her options. Two were pink with flowers, the third a cobalt blue with gold accents, and the fourth, a reddish-brown color with silver leaves.

Her first thought was the door, and her second was the hairbrush. Aris couldn't shake the image of the man with the gun and the crazed look in his eyes. *Monster.* That was the word that had immediately came to mind, but then, wasn't that the same word that had once been used to describe the owner of her ring? The shopkeeper, the break-in at the library, and now her locker . . . it was all the work of other Anathemians. Aris was beginning to question just what kind of people her ancestors were, and if the blood running through her veins was just as accursed as it had been all those years ago.

She selected the blue teacup and Lochlen reached for one of the floral ones—*thank god*. But even after the red cup was gone, Aris couldn't shake the thought of the color. She leaned forward, her voice low. "Why did our ancestors leave Krys—you know?"

"They were banished," Lochlen said plainly.

The server returned with two dark green teapots. He placed each one on a stone plate, warning them not to burn themselves before leaving again. Lochlen took a spoon of amber-colored sugar and added it to his cup, the smell of bergamot wafting from his pot as he poured.

"But what did they do that was so bad?" Aris pressed, filling her own cup.

"Assassins, thieves, traitors to the crown. Your guess is as good as mine." He said the words so easily, like he was listing off potential careers. "Here," he added, handing her a jar of brown sugar Aris hadn't noticed.

She set down the spoonful of white she was about to add to her cup and touched one of the suns on the bracelet she was now wearing. "Yours were definitely thieves," she said, perking up at the edges.

Lochlen smirked. "So you *do* like it."

Aris shoved her hand under the table. "I might've liked it better if you'd actually paid for it."

"Sorry I don't have a trust fund to charge it to," Lochlen said dryly then took a long sip of his tea as if to wash down the roughness. "But if it makes you feel better, I left something in its place. And who knows, they might even fetch a higher price for it than whatever they'd have gotten for that piece of junk."

Aris crossed her arms. "If it's such a piece of junk, why bother stealing it at all?" She dropped her gaze. "Unless . . . What did you do to it?" Aris stuck her arm straight out, as if it might explode. "This is some weird karma thing, isn't it? You know, you stole it, so now it's cursed, and you're sitting there just waiting for lightning to strike me down."

"That's ridiculous," Lochlen scoffed. "Besides, I hardly think the recompense for stealing a bracelet is lightning."

"Fine, you wear it then."

"What? no!" He recoiled, but it was too late. Aris dove across the table, nearly spilling her tea as she reached for his arm. Lochlen snaked his hand away just in time, but she lunged for the other one, sinking her nails into his sweater as she shook the bracelet from her wrist. Lochlen's hand flailed like an animal. "It's yours now. I gave it to you," he said as he flicked his wrist.

"Then you can give it back, once I know it's not going to kill me," she breathed, attempting to lock his fingers, but every time she thought she had the bracelet lined up, he broke free. The game went on like this until Aris's pace gradually diminished. She moved sluggishly now, heavy breaths giving way to laughter as she swayed with the jerk of his hand. Aris might've been stubborn, but Lochlen was relentless. Glancing up, she expected to see his eyes roll or his brows crease, but what she found instead was far more compelling. Lochlen was smiling. She blinked slowly between long, studying stares. Because the face in front of her was so different from the boy she'd come to know. His cheeks had color and his eyes almost seemed to glimmer. The gloomy boy looked more human than demon, more boy than prophet, more *dream* than nightmare. A memory was screaming at her now, pounding to be let in.

Lochlen relaxed his arm in her grip. He parted his lips as if to speak, but before he could get a word out, Aris grabbed his hand and slid the bracelet onto his wrist. His mouth hung open a moment longer while her own spread into a slow, triumphant grin.

He turned to the window, his head hung low, and when he turned back, the glimmer in his eyes was gone and the condescending smirk had returned. "Weird karma thing?" he said, jingling the bracelet.

"You never know." Aris shrugged. "Besides, you're not usually this"—she drew back, one of her brows raised—"*friendly*."

Lochlen sighed. "Maybe it's because you finally let me finish a cup of tea," he said, the last bit of amusement draining from his voice.

Aris rolled her head back. "Be serious."

"Oh, I'm being perfectly serious. English people never joke about their tea."

"So, how'd you end up in Elsley?"

"I was still half asleep when Mum brought out a map," Lochlen said, staring down at his cup. "Told me to close my eyes and point."

Aris took a long sip of tea. "Seems like an awfully big coincidence."

Lochlen shrugged. "If you believe in those."

Aris wasn't sure what she believed in anymore. It was hard to believe in anything after seeing a child die the way she had. Even harder knowing she had looked a bit like . . . like Evie.

She picked at a scab on the back of her hand. "Were you at my school today?"

"That's Alek's thing, not mine." Lochlen shifted his gaze. "Why?"

Her limbs felt hollow, but moving them seemed impossible. Aris expended the rest of her energy just to smooth a thumb over the tiny scratch that was now swollen and angry. "When you called me at lunch, well, I sort of lied."

"I know."

"How?"

Lochlen glanced out the window again, and she could see the faint glow of his reflection. He'd stopped blinking, but she couldn't see what he was staring at. "It felt like walking outside in the dead of winter. When it's so cold that your breath catches."

"And you thought of me?" Aris remarked, her chin dipping.

Lochlen sighed. "Not on purpose." If it weren't for everything else that had happened, Aris might've brushed it off. She might've let herself believe that the feeling had been because of Brent and the awkwardness at lunch. But the timing was too unsettling. Lochlen folded his arms. "Are you going to tell me what happened?"

When Aris explained the situation with her locker, part of her still hoped it was him and that he would eventually fess up. But he didn't. Instead, he rubbed a hand along his forehead. "Was anything missing?"

She bunched her hands in her sleeves, and then, in a feeble voice, she said, "You don't think someone—"

"Actually, I do."

"But how—why?" Someone had been in her school. They'd walked down her halls and rummaged through her stuff. Someone had been close enough to confront her if they'd wanted to. But they didn't. And the worst part of all this was none of it seemed logical. She felt like she was losing her mind, all of these little, seemingly meaningless things, a series of hunches. Each event on its own didn't seem that threatening, but as she strung them all together, the picture they made was like a giant neon sign, and it was telling her to run.

Lochlen pulled out his deck and laid four cards face up on the table: the Magician, the Eight of Cups, the Moon, and finally, the World. He was still wearing the bracelet as he touched a finger to the final card. "If you woke up tomorrow and Yuki had found the portal, would you come with us?" He ran a finger along the rim of his empty cup, waiting for Aris to answer. Waiting for her to say yes. But she didn't. Aris didn't say anything. Because going to Krysidia meant leaving everyone else behind. It meant leaving *Evie* behind.

CHAPTER 25

Aris had always been amazed by the fact that her hair looked worse just after brushing it. Although, tonight, it seemed that wasn't the case. She looked at herself in the mirror, at the strands that curled smoothly away from her face. Then she looked down at her hairbrush, eyes fixed on the silver handle. Had she always had this brush? Aris examined her reflection again, only this time, the door creaked open behind her.

The silver handle slipped from her hand as a figure strewn in shadows stepped soundlessly into view. Her stomach clenched and Aris was up before the hairbrush hit the ground. No, not now, not like this. The figure lunged and Aris rolled onto her bed. She made for the door, a breath caught in her lungs as she barreled into the hallway.

Florescent lights blared overhead, and she winced at the sound of locker doors being slammed. She could feel the figure behind her, could feel them catching up. Aris cursed under her breath. She didn't know where she was running to, only that it was getting harder. The more she pushed, the slower she moved, and like that wasn't enough, the hallways were littered with relics. A grandfather clock chimed as she tripped over a leather footstool. Scrambling to keep her balance, Aris veered to one side, following a corridor labeled "IV."

Lockers melted into bookcases as she ran. Where was Alek? And why had she gone to the library alone? Hadn't he warned her not to—something dug into her leg and Aris went down hard. She brought her arms up to shield her head as she landed, knowing it wouldn't be much use. Run or die. Those had been her options. She wasn't strong enough to fight, or at least not to win.

The corridor had led to a dark room that looked more like a study than a library, and as she shrank against the side of a couch, her breaths were loud enough to be screams. She pressed a hand to her mouth, only to realize the sound wasn't any quieter. Because it wasn't *her* breathing. Aris dragged herself away from the sound, slipping behind a massive wooden desk.

That was when she saw it: the door. It was dark red, almost brown, and slicked with a thick layer of blood. *The door to Krysidia*. Aris felt her chest expand. Her first thought was, *How could they not have checked the library?* Followed closely by, *Oh fuck*.

The breathing was getting closer, and she desperately reached for the knob, but it was no use. The portal was locked. "Please," Aris cried at last. "Please, someone . . . please, someone let me in." She pounded on the door, knowing it was her only chance, knowing that whoever rounded that desk was going to kill her.

The screech of metal silenced her sobs and a pair of eyes stared down at her from beyond the door. "Your kind aren't welcome here," a stern voice said, and then slammed the narrow hatch shut.

Her throat burned. She wanted to keep knocking, keep begging, but she noticed blood on her hands. They'd never let her in, not like this. Aris dropped her arms but kept begging, speaking now to her assailant. The figure stood at the edge of the desk, and Aris's next word came out very small, as small as she must've looked in a crumpled heap on the floor. "Why?" she whimpered.

Her assailant took a slow step forward and dropped their hood. The face beneath it was her own. And so was the hand that reached back and pulled out a gun. "We're Anathemians," the mirror version of herself said. "It's our nature." She twirled the weapon and with a half smirk, she pointed it at Aris. "Guns are so unfair," she mused.

And then she pulled the trigger.

When Aris opened her eyes, she couldn't move. Or maybe she could and just didn't want to. The door, the shooting. It had all been a dream. She knew that, but the fear was real. Her body ached. Her shoulders, her neck, her jaw . . . they were all still tensed. She attempted to turn her head, but it was like running frozen hands beneath a stream of hot water—the pain got worse before it got better.

She started with her toes, forcing them to flex before working her way up to her jaw. Aris pressed a hand to her cheek as she opened and closed her mouth. *Just a dream.* When she could sit up, she scanned her room, starting at one corner and working her way around until she noticed the pile of laundry on the edge of her bed: two stacks of perfectly folded sweaters.

It probably shouldn't have worried her as much as it did, only she knew for a fact they hadn't been there when she fell asleep, and Aris couldn't help but think back to her locker, to the neatly stacked textbooks. But of course, this wasn't the same thing. This was her bedroom, not her locker. There was no way anyone could—A noise echoed up from the first floor and her stomach somersaulted. Her first instinct was to run, but she remembered how well that had worked out in her dream. Instead, she grabbed her sharpest palette knife and crept downstairs.

When the sound of footsteps lingered outside the bathroom, Aris nervously confronted them. What happened next was a colorful string of curses followed closely by a spasm of lights. David had one hand pressed to his chest, the other raised against the tip of her palette knife. "Aris?"

Aris froze, looking between her dad and the knife, and then to her own blank expression reflected in the metal. "I-I heard a noise," she said breathlessly. "And then, the sweaters, and you"—she shook her head—"there was a pile of them on my bed and—"

"I know. I put them there. I didn't say anything because you were already asleep."

"Oh." Aris lowered the palette knife. "I thought it was someone else, that they'd gotten into the house or something . . ."

David's forehead creased. "You thought someone broke into the house to fold laundry?" Until then, Aris hadn't realized how ridiculous she sounded. She shrugged, both arms curling around her waist, and David gave her one of those looks, the kind parents give when they know something's wrong. But he didn't ask her about it just then. Instead, he rubbed the stubble on his chin and said, "How about a game?"

The game was janggi, and although they'd been playing since she was ten, Aris had never won a match. As David dusted off the board, she wasn't thinking about ways to beat him; she was thinking about ways to tell him the truth. About her ring and her powers . . . all of it.

The problem was, telling her parents meant there'd be a chance of Evie finding out as well. Aris dumped out a jar of flat tokens, collecting the ones marked with blue and leaving the red ones for her dad. She never did go back for that Sailor Moon clock. Not that she'd had much of a chance; Lochlen practically had to carry her out of the shop.

She sighed. She didn't know what she was so afraid of. It wasn't as if Evie would ever turn on her. But maybe that was exactly why Aris couldn't bring herself to tell her—because Evie wouldn't be upset, or at least not with Aris. Evie wouldn't blame her sister for being born first, but Aris almost wished she would. Because if she was honest with herself, she would admit that the real reason she didn't want to tell her sister was that then Evie would know that being first born didn't actually matter, that the ring would work for Evie just as it worked for Aris, and that the only thing preventing Aris from passing the magic along was her own selfishness.

Watching her father set up his tiles, Aris thought about her dream. She glanced down at her palms, half expecting them to be wet with blood.

Until now, Aris had thought there were two kinds of Anathemians: good ones, and bad ones. And until now, she *thought* she was one of the good ones, but she also thought there was nothing she wouldn't do for her sister. Maybe she was only good because she hadn't had a reason to be anything else. Maybe she wasn't a monster only because she wasn't hungry enough yet.

Suddenly, Aris was worried her nightmare had been more than just a dream. After all, prophets predicted the future, didn't they? What if looking for Krysidia was a waste of time? What if the word *banished* was as irrevocable as it sounded? And what if their quest was what ended up getting them all killed?

"Is everything okay?" David asked as he gathered his pieces.

"Everything's fine." Aris nodded a little too much.

It felt as if she'd been backed into a corner. She couldn't rely on Krysidia, she couldn't stay in Elsley, and she couldn't bring herself to tell her parents the truth. Every way out of this was dark and uncharted, and instead of charging forward blindly, she remained with her back against the wall, fumbling for a loose stone or a hidden lever.

Aris arranged her tokens and then moved her right soldier one point to the left. David did the same. "Have you ever wanted to live somewhere else?" she asked as she attacked his rook.

He countered with his cannon. "Are you thinking about university?"

Aris bit down on her tongue. "Yeah," she dragged out the word. "I thought maybe I needed a change of scenery." She studied the board, plotting her next move. "Don't you ever get sick of this place?" Her dad tilted his head as if she'd gone too far. She rushed to attack again, realizing too late that she'd left him an opening and David didn't hesitate to take it.

"When I graduated from high school, my parents had certain. . . expectations. They said I'd learned all I could in this town. I was supposed to go off and find greater waters or something." He watched Aris make her next move. "When I told them I wanted to stay, well, they were furious, to say the least."

"Did they ever forgive you?"

He rubbed one of his eyes and Aris realized he wasn't wearing his glasses. "Let's just say I'm pretty sure my sister is the golden child now. She seems to have fulfilled their dreams in my place."

As her father got up to make tea, she couldn't shake the feeling that his story was unfinished. At the same time, she was pretty sure she'd gotten her answer. And it wasn't the one she'd hoped for.

They played their next few turns silently. Aris took her time, savoring long sips of tea as she devised her next three moves. But every time she thought her dad had walked into one of her traps, it turned out she had fallen for one of his.

It killed her that she couldn't outsmart him. That planning three moves ahead was useless against a man who could formulate seven. She was a prophet, for god's sake. Shouldn't she be able to read his mind?

Prophets can't read minds. She heard the words in Lochlen's voice, and it reminded her of their conversation at the teahouse. Aris started thinking about her locker again and how tomorrow was an in-service day, so she wouldn't be back to check it until Monday.

Whoever had broken in could've taken anything or nothing. They could've straightened up unthinkingly or done it intentionally. Had they wanted her to know they were there? Aris was no closer to figuring it out than she was to discerning David's next move. And maybe it was stupid of her to try. Maybe there was no easy way out of this, no secret passage to slip through. She couldn't win, and she couldn't trick her parents into packing up and moving cities. The only option left was to surrender.

Aris set her mug on the side table. "Actually, there's something I've been meaning to tell you." She paused, noticing ten little toes where light from the kitchen stretched to the lower half of the stairwell. Evie.

Knowing her sister was listening made Aris's words stagger back down her throat, and what she ended up saying was something along the lines of "I've been dating this boy."

She was a coward.

Aris frowned down at her lap, completely forgetting she'd said anything at all until David lowered his mug and said, "Yes, the er"—he rustled his fingers together—"the British one."

"What?" Her head shot up as the word catapulted from her mouth. "No." She curled her hands into fists, kneading them into her thighs. "Definitely *not* the British one. Where did you even hear—" Her face flattened. "Ashton."

David tapped a finger against his mouth. "Yes, he said that you said this boy was"—he pinched his fingers together, as if conducting an orchestra—"quite pretty."

"I did not say that," Aris exclaimed. "I"—she let out a breath, mindlessly moving her rook—"it doesn't even matter, I just . . ." David made his next move before she could finish her sentence.

Unbelievable. Aris thought back to her skirmish with Lochlen. How she'd taken advantage of his being distracted to slip the bracelet onto his wrist, and how David had just used the exact same tactic to win the game. She almost laughed at how pleased her father looked with himself, mostly because she could've been staring into a mirror.

After finishing her tea and cleaning up the board, Aris turned to head back upstairs, stopping just short of the hallway. "His name's Alek, by the way." She wasn't sure if David had believed her story, but the name wasn't so much for him as it was for Evie; the toes were still on the edge of the step. Because if anything should happen, she wanted her sister to know she could trust Alek.

CHAPTER 26

Pulling up in front of Alek's house, Aris was reminded of how little she actually knew about his life. She was aware his grandfather owned a law firm, but as the two of them rounded the driveway, the five-door garage made her think the vintage Ambassador Alek borrowed was only one of many. In fact, if there was one word to describe the house in front of her, that would be it: many. Many doors, many windows, many turrets, and many professionally sculpted shrubs. It was the type of house that had a fountain in the center of the driveway, simply because it fit.

She'd forgotten to tell him she didn't need a ride to school this morning, and rather than letting her spend the day alone, Alek had brought her here. Not that she was complaining. Aris rolled her head to one side. "Which half is yours?" she asked, expecting him to laugh. But when she glanced back over her shoulder, he seemed almost embarrassed. She dropped her gaze, fingers searching for something to occupy them.

To her relief, Alek cleared his throat. "The top half," he said, indulging the affluence before pushing open his door. He made his way to a set of rounded steps and splayed out a hand. "So this here is the front of the house," he said, and Aris had barely begun to look when he moved on to the interior. She rushed to follow him through a massive set of doors that made the ones at the library seem modest. "That gate there takes you to the east wing," he continued. "The opposite one takes you to the west wing, and"—Alek flicked his wrist—"those stairs there coincidentally take you to the second and third levels."

The inside bore no trace of being lived in. It was eerily white with jewel tones sprinkled throughout, just enough color to keep the hallways from looking like an asylum.

"And this"—he pushed through another set of doors—"is the parlor." Alek took a seat in front of a window that stretched from floor to ceiling. "I'm not allowed in here anymore," he added, smirking a little, and Aris tried not to think about what he might've done to merit the *anymore* at the end of that sentence, but suspected it had something to do with the cabinet full of scotch.

The parlor was still mostly white, but gold accents made it feel softer than anywhere else she'd seen, not that he'd shown her much. But even with sunlight pouring in through the windows, this room still didn't feel like Alek. None of the house did. A tiny piece of her hoped the second and third floors were different, that when he'd said the top half was his, he'd meant it. But she had a sinking suspicion that was not the case, because if all those rooms were his, why would Alek have brought her to the parlor?

"I'm going to tell my parents the truth," Aris announced, taking a seat on an ornate sofa. "And wherever we end up going," she added, her voice not as strong as it started, "I want you to come with us."

"What?" Alek shook his head. He leaned forward, considering her words for a moment. "What about Krysidia?" he insisted.

Aris smiled weakly, her throat thickening as her hands slipped loosely into her lap. "We don't even know if it's real."

Alek held her gaze for a moment then bolted from the room, returning a few minutes later with an armful of papers. He spread them out, first across the tables, then on the couches and chairs, and finally across the floor. He rifled through pages until Aris was stranded on her cushion, surrounded by an ocean of handwritten notes.

"The writing at the ruins was Welsh, or at least part of it was," he said, his voice laced with caffeine. "Now, Celtic mythology tells of a race of supernatural beings called Tuatha Dé Danann, a.k.a.—"

"Faeries. Yeah Alek, I know, but—"

"Tuatha Dé Danann translates to *people of the goddess Danu*. Danu, who is known by some as the triple goddess." He turned to face her, one finger outstretched. "You remember the symbol at the ruins? The same as on our rings? It's the triple moon." He tapped the edge of one of the pages lining the coffee table. "The Tuatha Dé Danann ended up in Ireland because they'd been *banished* from heaven. And then, when they were chased out, they disappeared beneath the foothills. Except maybe they didn't just disappear." A pen rolled out from one of the piles, and Alek fiddled with it. "Did you know these beings were often described as having red hair? It's a pretty rare trait, and yet anthropologists have discovered red-headed mummies in central Asia, long before travel of that distance was feasible."

"But how does that—"

"The portals." He raised the pen in the air, using it to emphasize each word. "They must've left through the portals. There are meridians all over the world, remember? But when they arrived in Ireland, they were said to have come by ship, which means either they weren't aware of the portals yet, or they'd been barred from using them. But it also means Krysidia would have to be close by. In fact, Ireland was probably the first land mass they came across." Alek scrambled for an image. "Look at this map. History is filled with rumors of an island situated just west of Britain, but whenever anyone goes looking for it, they can't seem to find it." He lifted a brow. "Sound familiar?"

The ruins, Aris realized, although she didn't say it out loud.

Alek exchanged one sheet for another and began reading aloud. "Hy Brasil: a bountiful paradise where all who dwell are bestowed with a gift. Becomes visible once every seven years, but still cannot be reached." He grabbed another. "Antillia, the isle of seven cities: sands laced with gold. Vanishes when approached. Avalon," he continued, flipping the page around, "a place of abundance and home to nine sisters, each skilled in the art of magic. This one even mentions the island as some sort of magical gateway, which just goes to prove that—"

"Alek." Aris's voice came out tired, as if she'd been the one doing all the talking, and when he looked up at her, his eyes were alight, as if he had all the energy in the world. She was reminded of the model ship from the antique shop, and for a sliver of a second, she wanted to tell him to keep going. But she remembered what came after the ship: the hairbrush, the truth about her locker, the dream. She reached out a hand, and then she changed her mind, resting it against the arm of the couch instead. "Have you ever come across the word *Hiraeth*?" she asked, and then watched his features slowly deflate. Alek took a seat on the ground, his back limp against the chair frame.

Hiraeth: a deep, inborn sense of yearning; longing for a home that never was, a place we can never return to, or never existed.

His eyes were darker now, like she'd stomped out the flames. He tapped his pen against the floor, where a line of dark hardwood was visible between the chair and the rug. "I thought you said you believed me."

"I don't *not* believe you. I just—" Aris took a breath. "Even if we found it, what makes you think they'd let us stay? They banished us, remember? *Banished.*"

"They banished our ancestors," Alek corrected. He reached tiredly for a bundle of notes and held them out to her. "This is a collection of swords from 800 to 1000 CE. The blades are free of impurities, something that requires heating the metal to 3000 degrees Fahrenheit, and yet the technology required to do such a thing was believed to be developed during the Industrial Revolution, nearly a thousand years later." Aris slid the notes from his hand, flipping through a trail of dates and arrows that led to one giant question mark. "Even if you don't believe the legends, can you believe that Anathemians have lived among humans for at least that long? That there's nearly forty generations between us and the ancestors they banished. That at this point, we're probably more human than Anathemian anyway."

Even if you don't believe the legends. How did she get to this point? How did *she* become the girl who didn't believe in legends?

Alek pushed aside some papers and slid toward her. "Did something happen?" he asked, head resting against the arm of the sofa.

Yes, she thought. "No," she started to say and then lost the rest of her words. She knew there was no point in lying about it, but how do you tell a boy who can't be killed that you're afraid of dying? How do you tell a boy without a family that you're afraid of leaving yours behind?

You don't, she concluded. *At least, not directly.*

Aris told him about the vision from the hairbrush and worked her way to the locker; she thought about mentioning the dream as well, but he already looked so put off that she decided to stop there. The gears churned behind his eyes in a way that reminded her of the day they met, only as she watched them spin, Alek looked as if he kept getting stuck, and the first thing out of his mouth wasn't about the murder she'd witnessed or the stranger rummaging through her things. Instead, he furrowed his brow and said, "What were you doing at an antique shop?"

"Lochlen said I needed to practice reading objects."

Alek raised his chin, and as he lowered it in a slow nod, a chill snaked down Aris's back. "Does he know about the locker?"

Aris interlocked her hands, picking at one of her nails as she nodded. "Actually, I think he might've known about it even before I told him. When he called at lunch, he said—"

"You talked to him at lunch?" Alek glowered, the accusation an axe whirling through the air. She didn't like the stiffness in his voice or the way it turned the bile in the pit of her stomach into something heavier. Alek looked away, a hand dragging down the length of his face, and something tugged at Aris's insides, plucking them like the strings of an out-of-tune guitar. It was a strange sensation, so unlike anything she'd ever felt. She scoured the room, searching for a distraction, for something to shake the vexation from her mind before it consumed her.

Her liberation, as it turned out, was a painting. It extended across two full pages propped up against the back of a footstool and was one of the few things printed instead of handwritten. Right in the center was an image of a man sleeping beneath the entrance of a temple, surrounded by an assembly of women. "Is that supposed to be King Arthur?" she asked, her voice steadier than she expected.

Alek nodded. "In Avalon." His words lacked both the confidence and enthusiasm they'd had earlier, and Aris's throat itched, knowing she'd been the one to drain the elation out of him.

She slid from her chaise to the floor. "Did you know researchers have started x-raying old paintings? They do it to analyze the creative processes, but sometimes they find entirely different artworks beneath the original."

Alek relaxed a little. "Too bad that one's currently hanging in a Puerto Rican museum." He turned to face her, the tips of his ears reddening. Their noses were nearly touching. He drew back ever so slightly. "Listen, I know you're scared, and I know it's unfair of me to ask this, but Krysidia—it's not something I can give up on. Not yet, at least."

Even as Aris opened her mouth, she was unsure what she was going to say. Would she plead her case once more, or would she accede? But before she could get a word out, Alek ran a hand along the back of his neck and said, "There's something I haven't told you." He pulled out a letter and handed it to her. One look was all it took to discern. *This* was the letter from Alek's dad—the one he'd left alongside his ring. The pages were tearing where they'd been refolded too many times, and Aris held them with the same gentleness with which Alek had cradled her ring on the night he revealed his magic.

After scanning it through from front to back, all she could think was that he'd been right. At first glance, the letter looked long, but it felt like reading a novel in point form. She already knew most of what was written, but one part stuck out. One very important part that no one had thought to mention. Aris shot Alek a floundered look. "Your grandfather *met* a group of Krysidians?"

He ran a hand through his hair. "If you want to call it that."

She read through the fifth page of the letter again, because *met* really wasn't the right word. Alek's grandfather hadn't *met* a group of Krysidians, he'd been *captured* by them. "But I don't understand." She handed the letter back. "If they were offering to bring him to Krysidia, why did he fight?"

Alek refolded the pages and carefully tucked the letter back into the pocket of his jeans. "If my math is right, he would have already been married, and my great-grandmother would have been pregnant or just given birth. I guess he didn't want to abandon them."

Why did he have to use the word *abandon*? Aris was battered by a sudden wave of guilt.

"Yuki has this theory," Alek continued. "He thinks my powers work by deflecting threatening energies. Almost like a giant cosmic shield." With a finger, he traced the outline of his ring, the thick metal cast that held three black stones in a sort of triangle. "But if you think about it, the ruins kind of do the same thing. And if Krysidia works just like the ruins, maybe *that's* how it stays hidden." Aris didn't like where this was going. "I'm pretty sure they need us. Or at least, they need *me*." If that conclusion scared him, Alek didn't show it. Instead he turned to her, hands pressed together as if to pray. "Three more days, that's all I'm asking for. If we don't find anything new by the full moon, you can tell your parents everything. I promise."

They need him, she thought nervously. If that were true, wouldn't someone have come looking for them by now? But she remained silent, waiting for Alek to bring up the last part of the letter. The part he'd glossed over as if it didn't matter. But it did, it *did* matter, because Alek's grandfather hadn't just escaped from the Krysidians; he'd killed one of them. He'd *killed* another protector, which meant . . . Alek wasn't entirely invincible.

Aris hugged her knees to her chest, eyes darting over the parlor. The room was a complete mess, but at least now it looked more like Alek. It looked the way she imagined the inside of his head. If Lochlen's thoughts were all carefully filed away, Alek's were everywhere and all at once. His were a hundred pages of notes when all he'd really needed was a letter. Why had he bothered with the stories at all? She turned, leaning her cheek against her knee. "Why didn't you just show me the note from your dad?"

Alek shrugged, and his shoulder brushed against her own. "Maybe because I wanted the legends to be enough."

Of all the things he could've said, that one struck her the most. Here was this boy with powers that rivaled the gods' and a mind that transcended dreamers'. He'd stumbled into her life and reached out his hand. He'd offered to take her to another world and . . . and she would be an idiot to turn him down.

Her stomach fluttered, and she swallowed back a pair of wings while hooking her fingers into the fabric of his shirt. She wanted to go with him. She wanted to be the Wendy to his Peter Pan. She wanted to find Krysidia and not look back. She wanted . . . she wanted to kiss him. The light hadn't fully returned to his eyes, but there was a spark, and Aris yearned to stoke it.

She tugged him closer, her hand still buried in the soft linen of his shirt, and this time, Alek didn't shy away. When the air around them shifted, Aris wondered if it was one of those things specific to prophets, or if Alek had felt it too. She leaned into him, eyes dim and lips slightly parted.

The sound of a car door slamming resonated from the driveway, and fear struck like a hammer to her side.

Alek sprang up in a panic, and Aris kept her mouth shut, asking him a question with her eyes instead. "It's Stephen," he whispered. "You have to go." His words were calm, but it was as if he'd screamed them. He scrambled to collect his notes, shoving them beneath several couch cushions before darting into the hall. He led them down a corridor Aris hadn't seen. "Shit," he exhaled, trying a door handle that didn't want to turn. They looped back around, padding toward a set of stairs instead.

Her heart thudded as if it were twice as heavy as normal, and Aris realized it was because of Alek. His emotions were bleeding into her, linking their senses as if her sentiments were mirroring his own. She understood now; earlier, when she mentioned the antique shop, it had been the same. Her feelings had been *his,* and the ache in the pit of her stomach was an echo of Alek's reaction.

The sound of keys jangled eerily through the house and both of them stilled. They waited, listening to the sound of heavy footsteps squeaking against marble tiles, and when a set of doors opened somewhere on the left side of the house, Alek pulled her in the opposite direction. The two of them rushed down a large familiar staircase that opened up to the foyer, and Alek's relief flooded through her.

But then everything froze over again. Stephen stepped out from around the corner, holding the pen that Alek had been fiddling with earlier. The hoary man clicked it once, twice, and said, "I received a call from your principal today." His voice was gritty, and Aris imagined smoke trapped in his lungs from years of lighting cigarettes. "He said you've missed almost a week of school." Anger bubbled up beside her. It threatened to explode as Stephen stressed, "How do you expect to graduate from law school if you're already flunking grade twelve?" He tucked the pen into his pocket. "But I suppose we can discuss this later." Stephen loosened his tie, shifting his attention to Aris. She tried not to stare at the short scratch along his cheek as he said, "You must be his girlfriend."

"She's not my girlfriend," Alek said carefully. "And she was just leaving."

"You know, you remind me a bit of my daughter," Stephen added, looking her over in a way that made Aris want to take a step back; it was the kind of look she probably should've expected from a lawyer.

"She's *nothing* like your daughter," Alek growled, making Aris wonder if the comment had been intended as an insult. His words left a knot in her stomach. *Your daughter*, Alek had said. Not *my mother*.

They didn't wait to hear his grandfather's response. Instead, Alek grabbed her by the arm before bolting for the driveway, and when the massive door slammed shut behind them, Aris could've sworn her bones rattled with it.

The knot in her stomach lasted the whole way home, and when Alek pulled up in front of her house, all she got as far as a goodbye was, "I'll talk to you later."

As Alek's feelings dispersed and her own settled back in, Aris became overwhelmed with a new, sinking sort of feeling. She watched his car get smaller and smaller as it glided down the road until eventually it disappeared completely. For some reason, *later* felt very far away.

CHAPTER 27

KkeeerRIP. KkeerRIP. KkeerrRIP.

Harrison didn't know how many pages he'd torn, only that the sound of ripping paper seemed to quell some of his more destructive thoughts. Frowning down at his copy of *The Picture of Dorian Gray*, he grabbed the seven remaining chapters between his finger and his thumb and pulled. When the spine didn't give, he pulled again.

Again.

Again.

Again.

A tear dripped from his chin to the page, highlighting a single word: *useless*. The half-empty book slid out of his hands, dropping to the floor with a soft thud.

Finding Krysidia was supposed to be the easy part. He'd been so close as a child, or at least he thought he'd been. His journal was filled with maps, all different areas of Elsley, each with dots and lines, with circles scribbled around sights he'd meant to investigate but had been too far to get to by bike. From afar it looked promising, impressive almost, but upon further inspection, he realized how little evidence he'd actually had.

<u>Entry 9</u>
Location: Rotting tree stump at the edge of Wilbur Park
Observation: Lots of moths
Deduction: Possible beacon?

<u>Entry 17</u>
Location: Mailbox at the top of Landon Hill
Observation: Struck with a cold chill
Deduction: Potential ghost interaction

Harrison pushed a hoard of granola bar wrappers from the coffee table, revealing a larger, more accurate map of Elsley that he'd picked up from a gas station. His father's letters said the Krysidians had referred to him as "Son of Kendrick," which could be a term used interchangeably with "Anathemian," *or* it could have greater significance within the whole of Krysidian history. When Harrison was in university, one of his favorite professors had been a woman who specialized in Arthurian legends, and in one of his introductory classes she'd mentioned the name of a Welsh ruler: Cynyr Ceinfarfog, or Kendrick in English. In an early version of the legend, Kendrick was said to have been somewhat of a foster parent to King Arthur. Of course, none of this helped Harrison find the portal, but if it suggested some truth to the legend, then perhaps it was the best place to start.

He flipped through a cheaply bound disquisition, streaking the most useful pages with a blue highlighter before returning his attention to the map in front of him. It was unmarked, save for three red X's where his father claimed to have encountered the Krysidians.

How stupid he was to reject them, he thought, his tongue pressed to his cheek.

Leaning forward, Harrison tried to make out a street name, but his eyes refused to focus. He pushed up from the map, noticing a smattering of dark smudges on his fingertips where ink had transferred to his clammy hands. Hands that shook as he reached for a container on the edge of the table. He shoved a forkful of greasy noodles into his mouth. They tasted like day-old cabbage and sesame oil, but it didn't matter. He just needed something to cushion his stomach before pouring himself another cup of coffee.

He was on his way back with a full mug in his hand when he noticed the stack of papers beside the door. With a groan, he set down his coffee and swiped the blue highlighter from atop his research. Harrison sank to the floor beside the essays he'd promised to hand back on Monday, and although he was pretty sure it was still Friday, he knew the chances of him noticing them a second time were slim.

Not that it mattered. If all went as planned, he would be in Krysidia by next weekend.

Who was he kidding? Nothing ever went as planned.

Harrison reached for the first paper, scrawling a large B across the title page. He continued, alternating between Bs and B+s until he got to Garret's essay, on which he wrote a crisp A+.

A faint hum broke him out of his daze. His phone. Of course, as soon as he went to grab it, the buzzing stopped, leaving him aimless. He checked the couch first, then the wardrobe. Next the fridge, the top of the bookshelves, and behind the coffee maker. He opened every drawer in his desk and dug through jumbles of pens and pencils and highlighters. Beneath a stockpile of rubber bands, he found a thin wooden frame that read "World's Greatest Uncle." In it, a younger, scrawnier version of himself sat in a hospital chair, a pale-haired baby boy in his arms.

Harrison stared at the photo until he lost feeling in his fingers. He returned it to the drawer, tossing handfuls of rubber bands over the frame as if shoveling dirt over a body. When he could no longer see the word *uncle*, he grabbed his mug, pouring half the coffee into the sink before reaching for a bottle of whiskey. His phone was tucked behind the nearly empty bottle.

9:36, the screen read, and Harrison was shocked to learn it wasn't yet midnight. Of course, then he noticed the date. A blare of sunlight stung his eyes as he tugged at a nearby curtain, confirming that yes, it was, in fact, Saturday. 9:36 *a.m.*

He scrolled through a series of notifications, all from Garret, but it was a voice recording that piqued his interest. Harrison hunkered down on the couch, sipping his coffee as he pressed the phone to his ear.

"She's been acting ... different," said the first voice. "Asking about her parents, glued to her phone screen. She's never home anymore."

"She's a teenager. That's pretty typical behavior," mused the second.

"It's not just that. She's jumpy, verging on paranoid. I got up to use the bathroom the other night, and she nearly stabbed me with one of her palette knives."

"Well, you do sort of skulk. And besides, she has always struggled with mild anxie—"

"Ashton. She knows."

There was a brief pause. "Do you think she's said anything to Evie?"

"I'm not sure."

"We could ask her."

"Evie?"

"We know she can't lie about it."

"And if it turns out she knew nothing? We'd be forced to tell her everything. Tell them *both* everything."

"Would that really be so bad?"

The recording ended. It wasn't a lot to go off, but Harrison had filled in enough of the blanks. Aris had a younger sister, an extraordinary one. He chugged the rest of his coffee, wincing as he swallowed, and then with a flick of his thumb, he deleted the voice memo.

What Brax doesn't know won't hurt him.

CHAPTER 28

Lochlen couldn't move right away. He couldn't feel the mattress cradling his back or the blanket bunched up at his toes. He couldn't feel anything. But he could scream. And he was. Lochlen was screaming because he could be awake just as easily as he could be asleep, and he wasn't sure which was worse. He was screaming because he didn't know what he could trust—certainly not his window, or his sheets, not the closet door he could've sworn he'd left open, and not the figure currently pinning his arms against the bed. "It's okay," the figure coaxed. "Lochlen, look at me. It was just a dream."

Just a dream. Lochlen clung to the words like a life raft as he waited for the storm clouds to clear in his head. He recognized Wyatt's eyes first.

His brother's irises were the same deep blue as their father's, and with a hint of stubble shadowing his jaw, he looked just like him.

Lochlen must've stopped screaming at that point because his brother released his arms.

"I'm sorry," Wyatt breathed. "I thought it would be better this way. If I had known what it would do to you . . ." Remorse hit Lochlen like a rock, dragging him down into its waters. He hated remorse more than most other emotions, especially when *he* was its focus. Lochlen didn't quite understand how it all worked, but somewhere in that twisted mess of emotions, he felt like running. *Fast and far.*

Lochlen walked to the bathroom to splash some water on his face, avoiding the mirror as best as he could. He didn't puke this time, but he wanted to, and when he returned, his brother handed him a glass of water that might've been cold at some point but was now tepid as he chugged it.

"Do you want to talk about it?"

Lochlen shook his head.

Wyatt used to argue, but now he just took the empty glass and made for the door. He always left it ajar in case Lochlen changed his mind, but he never did. Instead, he nudged the handle, closing himself off from his brother, from the rest of the house, *from the world.*

He fell back against his bed, no longer afraid of his sheets, but nervous nonetheless. Once upon a time, he had to write out everything he could remember of his dreams. He used to have lists of symbols and an entire shelf of journals. But now his subconscious did most of the work for him. Now waking up was like waiting for the dust to settle, for the water to become clear. And now that it had, Lochlen wanted to hurl a stone into the lake and stir it all back up.

Wind whistled. A long, low howl that made the hairs stand on the back of his neck. Lochlen rose from his bed, slowly craning his head until his window became visible in his peripheral. Seeing the sash upraised turned his sweat to ice. It was the same feeling he had at the shop, like someone was watching him.

Lochlen drew himself to his feet, careful not to lose sight of the window. It was three paces from the edge of his bed to the open sash. He held his breath as he moved.

One.

Two—The feeling dissolved.

He let himself exhale.

Three.

Whatever—whoever had been there left no trace, save for the open window, which Lochlen promptly shut and locked. He leaned back, knocking his head against the wall as the realization sunk in.

He should've known the reaper was shady, that an article like that wouldn't just show up on his feed. And he should've gotten everyone out of that damn shop the moment he sensed a second presence. But he'd been selfish.

He pressed a hand to the window, welcoming the bite of cold glass against his bare skin.

Love is weakness. It was a line usually delivered by villains, and yet he was beginning to understand its basis. From the moment he'd seen her through the window of Alek's car, he'd lost all sense of primacy. His instincts used to be sharp enough to stab a person, but now they were nothing more than a dull murmur in his ear.

He shoved a pile of books from his desk, and they went hurtling across the room. Six lives. That's what he'd risked to learn more about the accident, to learn more about her parents. He'd wanted that for her, for Aris. He'd wanted it so badly and now . . . now they were all about to suffer the consequences.

Lochlen reached for his father's watch, but in its place was the bracelet. A dainty little thing with too many suns and not enough stars. He leaned back, resting his head against the wall. Closing his eyes, he pictured the frivolity in her expression as she fought to slip it onto his wrist. By the time she started to laugh, he hadn't even cared that she was rejecting his gift because in that moment it was as if nothing had changed, as if he was the boy who made her sleep on the rug, and she was the girl who painted stars on his cheek while he rested. As if she remembered all of it.

He feared that their time together was just another dream, that he would wake up with yet another memory of her that she wouldn't have of him. Even now, if he hadn't been wearing her bracelet, if his father's watch wasn't gone, he might still be lost in speculation.

There's this feeling you get in a dream, like your mind is lagging a few seconds behind your body, as if it's a balloon being pulled along by a string. Lately, he'd been feeling that way a lot, regardless of whether he was asleep.

With a hand pressed to his cheek, Lochlen closed his eyes. He traced his fingertips along the edge of his jaw and let his eyes roll back. He blinked, slowly and then quickly, trying each movement as if test-driving a new car. He wanted to pick the motion that handled the smoothest, but neither of them gave any hint of normalcy. He sat on his bed, and on his floor; he looked out the window at the moon that was almost full. And then, finally, his gaze defaulted to the bracelet again.

Guilt wormed its way into his chest, carving out the relief that had been there, that had come from knowing their day together had been real. *Was it worth it? Was a moment of laughter really worth whatever nightmares she'll endure from finding that hairbrush?* Objects like that were the reason he hated attending estate sales, but he'd been to that antique shop a hundred times . . .

Lochlen bent down to collect the books he'd scattered across the room. He shouldn't have sent her off on her own. He let a book slip from his hand. It hit the floor with a thud and Lochlen sank down to join it.

Why was it that every time he was with her, Aris ended up in some sort of distress? First, the license plate; then he'd nearly poisoned her at the ruins; then the reaper at the shop, not to mention her mother's spirit imploding right before her eyes; and now, the hairbrush. He was beginning to understand why he'd needed to stay home that first night, why Aris didn't remember him. He was bad for her, even when he was trying to be good.

Where the relief had been, and then the guilt, now there was nothing. Nothing but a gaping hole, a cavern in the center of his chest, and Lochlen had to hunch forward with his hand around his neck because his head ached now too.

He refused to sleep, and he was being punished for it. It was like all his dreams were stuck inside his skull, pounding to be let out. But he didn't want any more visions of the future. What he really wanted was to go back in time for a moment. He wanted to run through the garden of his old house, to lie down under the shade of an ash tree and count the leaves. If only he could capture a dream as easily as a photo could preserve a memory. Then he could go back whenever he wanted. *Then*, all he'd have to do was hand Aris a locket or a key or a bracelet, and she'd remember everything.

Lochlen snatched his deck from beneath his pillow and placed four cards face up in front of him: the Magician, the Eight of Cups, the Moon, and finally, the World. The Magician signified success; the Eight of Cups a time for transition. The Moon he suspected was more of a literal translation, and finally, the World: fulfillment of one life, the start of the next. A few weeks ago, Lochlen had dreamt of these four cards. They'd repeated over and over, filling his entire deck, their meaning clear as day. By the next full moon, he and his friends would find their way back to Krysidia. The signs that followed had almost felt forced. A series of phone calls from an unregistered area code. Books constantly falling open to specific pages. The puzzle was there, waiting to be solved. But Lochlen hadn't been ready to decipher it. He hadn't been ready to leave—*hadn't been ready to give up on her.*

Now that they'd been exposed, he knew the portal was their only option, but he also knew Aris wouldn't come with them, that she wasn't willing to leave her family behind for some kids she'd met two weeks ago. But maybe if she knew the truth, if she remembered him, if she realized he wasn't a stranger . . . maybe she'd change her mind.

The memories were there. They were lingering right beneath the surface. They had to be. Because every so often one of them would slip out. It was a single bubble floating to the surface—a candlestick holder pointed right at his eye. It couldn't have been a coincidence, Aris grabbing *that* of all things. He'd felt ten years younger in that moment, and his seven-year-old self wanted so badly to shake her awake. The truth had been building in his chest and Lochlen had scrambled to patch up every leak before the words flooded out of him, sweeping away every new memory and letting the old one settle between the cracks.

But would seven years of dreams really change the way she saw him now, or would any of it even matter?

He thought about the dream he had the night he'd stayed home from the party. How he'd gone to sleep only to find someone clawing their way inside his head. And then he remembered the solace he'd felt when she fell into his arms—not just his, but hers as well. "Found you," she had whispered, as if it was all just a game. And maybe to Llewellyn, it was.

Lochlen gathered his cards, shuffling them over and over. Usually when he woke up screaming, it was because of a nightmare, but tonight it had been because of a dream. For three years he'd had visions of his best friend descending into darkness, watched him bring pain onto others in a desperate attempt to expel his own. He'd watched Alek's rage give way to chaos, witnessed what his powers could do with the wrong motivation, and seen what remained of the world when he was done. And for three years he'd tried everything to keep those nightmares from crossing over, to keep his best friend from treading too close to the edge, to keep him from slipping . . .

But now, he'd been offered a solution. Lochlen had begged Llewellyn for an alternative, for a way that didn't involve losing Aris, but he'd burned her name into a bench and now she was punishing him by giving Lochlen exactly what he'd asked for. Llewellyn had shown him a future, one she knew he would never pursue because it meant betraying the very friend he was trying to save.

If Alek lost his magic, he'd lose his ammunition. If Alek lost his magic, he'd never return to Krysidia. If Alek lost his magic . . . it'd make Lochlen's job a hell of a lot easier. Not that he was actually considering it.

Unless . . . maybe he was?

If his instincts were wailing, Lochlen couldn't hear them. Instead, he heard Aris's laughter, saw her smile, felt her hand in his. Lochlen straightened his deck. *Love is weakness,* he thought again, this time wondering whether betraying a friend to protect the world would make him a villain, or a hero.

CHAPTER 29

Alek wasn't invincible in video games. Just like anyone else, he had a certain number of hit points and once they were gone, so was his avatar. But at least when he died in a game, he knew he deserved it.

Currently, he was hiding in a bit of shrubbery, chugging a healing potion while battling a giant lizard whose hide was worth twice as much as all his gear combined. He knew he should be helping Yuki re-examine their notes, that if they didn't find Krysidia in the next two days, everyone was going to leave, that *Aris* was going to leave. And he also knew how naïve it was to get worked up over a girl he'd just met, but maybe that was exactly why he was so afraid of letting her go. Lochlen, Jada, the twins . . . their bonds ran deep, a hundred strands of braided steel forged from a hundred moons' worth of memories. But for Aris, those ties were just beginning to form. Her strands were spun from cotton and Alek clung to her by threads. If she left right now, there was a chance they wouldn't stretch, and once they snapped, that would be it. Alek would never see her again.

Cheering erupted through his headset as Alek landed a direct hit. The lizard left itself open to attack, and he and the second half of his party pelted it mercilessly, he with his sword, and she with magic.

It was still eight months before he turned eighteen, and although Aris had offered to take him with her, he knew Stephen would never allow it. In fact, Stephen was rich enough that the only place Alek could go and not be found, the only place he could hide, was one that Stephen didn't know existed. One he couldn't see.

Alek cursed as his hit points took a sudden dive, but in video games, surviving wasn't a given—it was a challenge. There was an exhilaration that came from knowing no one was looking out for his avatar, that one misstep was all it would take to lose everything—or at least everything he was carrying. Ignoring the shouting in his ear, Alek ran back to town to restock his potions and switch over his sword. As he scrolled through his inventory of weapons, one stuck out to him. Excalibur. Ironically, it was one of his weaker swords, the kind any mid-level player earned from completing enough quests. But in proper myth, Excalibur wasn't just a weapon, it was a symbol of true worthiness. A sword of magic said to protect its wearer from injury. *Not unlike his ring.* Maybe that was just another coincidence.

With a rucksack full of swordfish, Alek trudged back toward the wilderness. How many of his theories had Aris actually believed, or at least wanted to believe? He knew she was scared, but he couldn't help but think that if Stephen hadn't come home when he did, he might've gotten through to her. If only he'd had the chance to show her the rest of his research . . . but Aris hadn't been looking at his notes when the car door slammed. She'd been looking at him, and if Alek hadn't scrambled to hide his papers and rush her from the parlor, Aris might've kissed him.

Aris might've kissed him.

Before then, he hadn't given it much thought, but in that moment, he would've given her anything and everything. He would've gotten in his car and driven halfway across the world. He would've marched back to that shop and threatened the reaper for answers. *He would've kissed her.*

"You bastard," shouted a voice in his ear, and Alek trailed back to find his partner's life nearly drained.

He cast a weak spell, hoping to shift the lizard's attention. "Sorry. I didn't mean to take so long." What followed was a colorful string of curses cut off by dead silence. Everything went dark. His screen, his computer, his lights . . . even his phone stopped charging.

Alek let out an exasperated growl. Apparently, it didn't matter that he'd spent last night obeying Stephen's every command, that he'd weeded the back garden and cleaned out the gutters. It wasn't enough that he'd scrubbed down all five bathrooms and squeegeed over a dozen windows. Nothing would ever be enough, especially after getting caught with Aris. "You remind me of my daughter," Stephen had said to her, but Alek knew the comment was intended for him, that what Stephen really meant was, *You will ruin her life, just like your father ruined your mother's.*

Alek thundered down to the study. It wasn't fair. He grabbed two bottles of overpriced rum, resisting the urge to hurl them across the room as he set off for the kitchen. He hadn't asked to be born, and yet Stephen punished him for it. The man had fought for custody just to keep him away from his father and then complained about having to raise him. Alek dumped both bottles down the sink and refilled them from a jug of apple cider vinegar. As he wafted a lighter over their lids to reseal them, he thought—just for a moment—about burning the whole godforsaken house to the ground. Instead, he gripped the lighter even tighter, forcing himself to take a deep breath.

Cruel inconveniences, that was what he called them. Anything more and he'd give Stephen a reason to retaliate, but anything less and, well, sometimes less wasn't an option. Because sometimes his head felt like it was going to explode. Sometimes, when his fingers curled, he wished it was around the hilt of a knife.

Alek slipped the bottles back into their slots then spent the rest of the afternoon resetting the clocks. The house had an unsettling amount of them, and when he was done, each one was a few minutes ahead of the next. After that, he took to scribbling unpleasant words across the floors, making sure his white marker was just barely visible. Stephen's eyesight was getting worse, and Alek hoped he would catch a reflection for a second, and then lose it. He hoped the man would see a word that wasn't there and think he was losing his mind.

But it still wasn't enough. Nothing would ever be enough. Not for either of them. Not while Stephen hated Alek's father for ruining his daughter, and not while Alek hated Stephen for chasing away his dad. Not while Alek's powers still protected him from harm, and not while Stephen was intent on using them against him. The man didn't have a clue about Alek's ring and yet, time after time, he'd been Alek's reason for wanting to take it off.

A bruised cheek can heal, he thought. *God. Spirit. Angel. Why do they care so much about my body? And why are they so willing to sacrifice my mind?*

He caught the edge of his reflection in a silver vase. His mind could've been beaten and shattered and bleeding out on the side of the road, and no one would notice. All they would see was silky hair and unmarked skin. They would see a boy with a big house and a fancy car, and they would call him ungrateful.

It wasn't fair, he thought, on his way to cut the pockets out of Stephen's dress pants. He was in one of the closets when he noticed the picture frame perched beside a collection of watches. In it, a little girl who he could only assume was his mother was waving a bright pink bubble wand. But it wasn't her smile that made the blood rush to Alek's ears. It was Stephen's.

Stephen, who never laughed, who never smiled, who spent weekends at his office when he had a house with twelve empty rooms.

It wasn't fair, Alek thought again.

That his mother had taken Stephen's love and ran, that she'd left them both angry and alone while she was off living a completely different life. Of course, Stephen had blamed him for that, too.

If you'd been a better son, she would've come back for you.

It wasn't fair.

It wasn't fair.

Alek threw the frame to the ground, reveling in the destruction as the sound of glass shattering licked his ears.

It wasn't—*enough*.

CHAPTER 30

I'll talk to you later. That had been the last thing Alek said to her, and now Aris worried they would be his final words. It had only been twenty-four hours since he had dropped her off, twenty-three since she'd texted to ask if he was okay, and twenty-two since Aris had started weaving worst-case scenarios in her mind. And it was for that reason and only that reason that she'd ended up on the front steps of Lochlen's townhouse.

She spent several minutes talking herself into and out of ringing the bell, only to end up knocking, and when an unexpected face greeted her at the door, Aris staggered back, nearly tripping over her own feet. The prince wasn't as colorful as the last time she'd seen them, but they'd all become a bit grayer since the incident with the shopkeeper. Today, the brightest thing about them was a blue satin scarf they used to tie back their long hair.

She double checked the number on the mailbox. "Isn't this"—her eyes refocused—"never mind. Is Lochlen with you?" She hadn't expected her voice to waver, but seeing Jada had thrown her off.

"He's still asleep," Jada said, slipping the door shut behind them. They took a small step forward, arms reaching out to take her hands before they thought better of it and folded them over their stomach instead.

"It's Alek. He . . . I don't know what happened, but he's not responding to my texts. I've called and got no answer. I stopped to check the ruins on my way over, but he wasn't there. I even—" Aris stopped herself before she completely broke down. "Have you heard from him?"

Jada's eyes darted from side to side. "I talked to him on Thursday, but . . ."

"But what?"

"He didn't show up at school yesterday."

"No, yeah." She fluttered a hand. "He was with me." Jada's head tilted to one side and she explained the situation: how Stephen had come home early and found them, and that Alek was skipping school and he wasn't allowed in the parlor for some reason. As Aris worked herself into a panic, thinking that Alek had somehow been captured while trying to avoid his grandfather, Jada's shoulders relaxed.

They leaned over a railing with more rust than paint as the neighbor looked up and waved. The woman had a pair of children flopped beside her, drawing stars on the driveway with a stick of blue chalk, and Aris's eyes couldn't help but brighten. Jada offered them a warm smile and waved back. "Why don't we go for a walk?" they said to Aris.

"A walk?" And just like that, her eyes darkened again. "I just told you your best friend is missing, and you want to go for a walk?" Jada pressed their lips together and Aris noticed that the oldest child had turned to stare at them. "I'm sorry," she added, lowering her voice. "I'm just . . ."

"On edge?" Jada offered, twisting back around, and this time they grabbed her hand. Their voice dropped to a murmur. "Mirai and I stopped for bubble tea the other morning, and I actually had to talk her out of bringing her katana inside." A weak laugh escaped their throat, but Aris could see the tension in their eyes.

She agreed to the walk, and for a while, the two of them sauntered in silence, Aris teetering along the curb and Jada beside her on the road, one arm slightly raised in case she lost her balance. She expected them to talk more, and maybe they'd expected the same from her. Of all Alek's friends, Jada was the one she'd spent the least amount of time with, and it only just occurred to her that they might not be as outgoing as they looked. Or at least, not without Mirai to coax them out of their shell.

The path Jada led them down was worn into the grass—the kind formed through years of passing feet—and as Aris trudged through brown leaves to a desolate playground, she couldn't help but question why, on a Saturday afternoon, not a single child was here swinging from the monkey bars. It was Alek she thought of then, the boy with an impossibly large house but not a home, the boy who walked through a marble-floored foyer that looked like a playground devoid of children. And for the first time since Aris had met him, she thought of Alek not as a brightly shining sun, but as a dwarf star drifting through space, sixty-four million kilometers from the nearest planet.

"I need you to tell me why you're not freaking out about Alek." She dragged her foot through the pit of gravel that was supposed to keep kids from ending up in the emergency room. "And don't say it's because of his powers, because I know what it said in the letter. I know he's not invincible." Jada took a steeling breath. "What if someone found him?" she pressed. "Just like they found his grandfather?"

"You mean if a group of Krysidians offered to take him to the portal, thus fulfilling our lifelong dream?"

Aris rolled her head back. "Be serious."

"I am being serious," they protested. "That's like the best-case scenario right about now." Jada took the metal steps two at a time, bounding to the top of the play structure. Aris chased after her, but as she reached for the railing she heard an odd yet familiar chirp. With her head slightly ducked she turned, eyes darting to the sky. She recognized the creature circling above the playground; it was the same one she'd seen outside The Twisted Juniper, and now that she thought about it, she was pretty sure she'd seen it in the mountains as well. Except, having had a better look at the thing, she saw that it wasn't a black bird at all. It was a bat. *What the hell is a bat doing out in the middle of the day?*

"Aris, wait," Jada cried, as Aris propelled herself up the steps, but their words were an afterthought as something sliced into her palm.

It took a moment for the blood to surface, and even longer for Aris to process what had happened. Last to catch up was the pain, but the instant it did, it became all she could think about. The more she stared at the gash, the deeper the sting, but she couldn't seem to look away. Jada was by her side in an instant. They tugged the scarf from their hair and wrapped it around her hand to stop the blood. They held their hands out flat, pressing them against her wound, one above and one below. "This is going to feel a bit weird, okay?"

What is that supposed to mean? Aris opened her mouth to ask when what felt like a bolt of electricity coursed out through Jada's fingers. At first it was like shaking awake a foot that had fallen asleep, but then the tingle became an itch, and holy shit did she want to scratch it. She squirmed in their grip, eager to sink her nails into her own skin, but Jada tightened their hold. "Shhhhh," they coaxed. "I'm almost done."

"Done what?" Aris squirmed again, but the itch was already fading. Jada released her hand, and she could see where her blood was soaking through their scarf. It turned the once-brilliant shade of blue a muddy purple, and Aris swallowed back a bitter tang that found its way into her mouth. The edge of the railing looked as though it had been doused with acid, and she now understood the lack of children.

Well, that's definitely going to need a tetanus shot.

But her wound no longer stung, which made Aris really worried. Maybe it was the adrenaline. Or maybe she'd sliced through all her nerves and ruined the hand she needed to hold a paintbrush. With a breath caught in her throat, Aris pinched one of her fingers, relief forcing the air from her lungs at the prick.

But the relief did nothing to quell her confusion, and she looked to Jada before carefully unwrapping the scarf. Blood still stained her palm, but it was dry now. Aris swallowed, pushing away the mass of nightmares prompted by the sight. She flexed her fingers, expecting to see the length of the cut well with a fresh line of red, but she couldn't even see where the laceration began. She rubbed at the surface of her palm until the sweat from her fingertips began wiping it clean. Working her way across like an archaeologist brushing away sand, Aris found nothing but a thin scab. She blinked up at Jada in disbelief, and they let out a small sigh. "Alek didn't tell you about my powers, did he?"

Aris shook her head. "I, uh"—she pointed to her palm—"am I still going to need a tetanus shot?"

Laughter bubbled up from Jada's throat, and soon they were overflowing with it. They threw an arm around her shoulder, steering her back down the steps and away from the hazardous playground. "That won't be necessary," they drawled. "But we should probably get back to Lochlen's house, if anything, to see if I can salvage this before the stain sets in." Jada examined both sides of the scarf before folding it into a square the size of their palm.

"Sorry." Aris grimaced a little, but Jada waved her off. As the park faded into the distance, Aris took one last look for the bat she'd seen earlier. But the skies were as desolate as the playground. Had she imagined the whole thing?

It didn't take long for Jada to explain their powers. "I'm a healer," they said, which pretty much summed everything up, although they made a point of saying they couldn't heal everything, and they told her not to go off and get herself killed thinking they could bring her back. Jada drew their hair behind one ear, revealing a trio of copper beads strung between two green stones. One was large and flat, set into an ornate medallion, while the second was smaller and dangled freely from their lobe.

Aris looked back down at her hand. She was starting to think rare didn't necessarily mean useful. Because compared to Mirai, who could rip a padlock in half, and Yuki, who could read thirty languages, and now Jada, who had just healed a wound in seconds that would have taken weeks to recover on its own, Aris's ability to sense objects seemed relatively inferior.

"So why are we going back to Lochlen's?" she asked, to which Jada held out the scarf. "No, I mean, why were you at his house if he was still asleep?"

Jada looked down at the scarf as if staring at a blood-soaked kerchief was more appealing than looking her in the eyes. They said, "I live there."

Aris forced herself to stare straight on, and she missed the curb on her next step. She toppled sideways, and Jada reached out a hand to steady her. Their arm was still entangled with her own when they told her about their mother, that she left a few years ago. Aris should have been shocked but she wasn't, which made her stomach churn. There was a pattern of Anathemians losing their parents.

"Now, before I tell you about my father," Jada continued, "just know that he's not a bad person."

Her arm fell away from theirs, and Jada let it. She considered reaching out to them again but ended up nodding instead.

"My mom never told him about her powers, so as you can imagine, he was pretty startled to find out about mine." They closed their eyes for a moment. "I knew he wasn't exactly open-minded, which is why I never planned on telling him, but last year . . . Well, he was up on the roof trying to replace a shingle when the wind picked up. It was strange really, because the skies had been relatively calm and then, out of nowhere, this massive gust ripped through the trees." Their eyebrows cinched together, as if they were still scouring for answers. "When he fell, I didn't even think. His leg was broken, I mean, really brutally broken, and he was losing a lot of blood." Jada looked away from the scarf now.

"So I healed him." They shrugged. "And after that, he couldn't even look at me."

For all her apprehension about telling her dads, not once did Aris consider that they might not accept her gift. Of course now, that worry shot to the top of her list. *He's not a bad person.* Jada's words repeated in an endless loop, and she looked up at them with a mix of sympathy and dread.

"Lochlen's brother had just started university, so they had an extra bed, is all. I mean, not all. His mom has been really good to me," they clarified. "Too good. Sometimes I feel guilty for letting them take me in. I mean, living with my dad was getting difficult, but like I said, he's not a bad person. He just . . . thinks I'm possessed by the devil." Jada shrugged again.

Aris jerked her chin. "That's ridiculous."

"Oh I know, right? If anything, I'm the opposite. I mean, I'm a healer. How could I even use that for evil? In fact, if any of us were possessed, it would definitely be—" They bit down on their lip, and she knew they were talking about Alek.

"Jada." They tried to keep walking, but Aris grabbed their arm. They didn't fight, but they didn't look at her, either. Instead, they stared at the ground, tapping their toes together. "If he's in trouble . . ." Aris pressed.

"He's not," Jada assured. "At least, not the kind you're thinking."

Aris released their arm. "I could still help."

"You can't help him. Trust me."

Jada started walking again, their pace eager, and Aris rushed to keep up with them. They were almost back at Lochlen's now, and she was worried that the minute they arrived, Jada would run inside and she would be left with more questions than she came with. She darted forward, cutting them off. "Listen, the night I met him, Alek saved me." She said the words without shame this time. "If something's wrong, then I have to at least try to help."

With a stiff voice, Jada relented, "The thing you need to understand about Alek is that he can't control his powers the way most of us can. He can't just turn them off. That means he lives in a constant state of fear, never knowing when something might happen or who's going to take the fall for it." With a slight tilt of their head, they added, "Sometimes I think the guilt is just . . . too much for him to handle."

"Jada," Aris panted. "Where is he?"

"I . . . I don't know." Jada wrapped their arms around themself. "Honestly, he could be anywhere. It's like he just disappears for a few days."

Her shoulders stiffened and dropped as a weight in her chest dragged her forward. She'd been so unbelievably selfish, going to Alek for comfort every time she had a bad day and expecting him to save her again and again. Attempting to talk him out of a dream he'd been chasing for half his life and all because of a nightmare. Aris drew her hands so far into her sleeves, she could've tied the extra fabric in a knot. It had never even crossed her mind that Alek might've struggled with his powers as much as she did with her own. *I never even asked.*

"I'll find him." Lochlen's words were a heavy door slamming into its frame, and Aris realized they were back at the house. Gone were the children with their chalk and she didn't blame them because dressed in black from head to toe, pressed against the railing like a raven trapped inside a cage, Lochlen looked like absolute hell. *I'll find him*, he said again, this time staring directly at her. And there was something about seeing the dark circles beneath his eyes and the clump of matted hair poking out from the edge of his hood, something about the way Jada had spoken that made her piece it all together. She understood now that this was it. This was what it was going to take to get Alek back.

Lochlen.

And absolute hell.

CHAPTER 31

There were a couple of places Alek liked to go when he was in a bad mood, and none of them were very nice. Lochlen had already checked the alley that people didn't always make it to the end of, and the park where fires were sometimes set. And when he'd stepped off the bus, half a block down from a dodgy pub on the south side of town, the driver had given him a look that said either, *Are you sure you know what you're getting into, kid?* or, *What do you think you're up to, hooligan?* Lochlen's answer to both was, *I have no idea.*

He wandered down the sidewalk and flashed the bouncer Wyatt's ID. While the resemblance between him and his brother was negligible at best, he was pretty sure he could've held up a credit card and still been waved inside.

Hit with a blare of lights in clashing shades of red and purple, and the ripe scent of sweat mixed with rum, Lochlen dragged a hand down the side of his face. He'd had too much sleep and not enough rest, and he was definitely *not* in the mood for this. Last night, when he'd been too tired to keep fighting his visions, he'd finally closed his eyes, only to have them shoot open a few minutes later. It was as if his mind was running through scenarios, using his dreams to test each outcome until he found one he could live with.

The music was barely audible over the constant chatter. Lochlen pushed his way to the bar and the man behind the counter bared his teeth. Lochlen glanced down the line for Alek and then ordered whatever was cheapest. *Alek had better be here*, was all he could think. *And he'd better have a car.* Lochlen shoved his last dollar into his pocket, knowing it wouldn't be enough for the bus ride home, and then grabbed the beer he had no intention of drinking before plunging back into the crowd.

Normally, at a place like this, Alek would've stuck out like a shiny quarter in a sack of old pennies, but tonight the tavern was definitely breaking some sort of fire code, and Lochlen could barely keep track of his own limbs.

The noise.

The smell.

The complete disregard for personal space.

If one more person rubbed their sweaty back against his arm, he was going to throw them through a window.

Shit.

Lochlen stumbled backward. The sound of glass cracking snapped him out of a daze, and he gasped. Beer pooled around his shoes—the bottle he'd been holding was in pieces on the ground. Not that anyone else seemed to care or even notice.

That was close. Too close.

Because after ten years of knowing him, it was not Alek's powers that frightened him the most. It was his rage. It was nights like this, reminding Lochlen of just how easily his nightmares could blur into reality. He tugged at the collar of his hoodie. *Alek is here alright.*

Jada, Mirai, and Yuki had all seen what Alek could do at his worst, but not what he was holding back. Lochlen, on the other hand, could see everything. If Alek's anger was a color, it would be black, not red, and when it was out of control, it enveloped him like flames. Just now, Lochlen had barely escaped one of its tendrils, but it worked like a magnet, luring him forward, hoping to claim two souls instead of one. Every time he'd been trapped in it, he ended up with blood on his hands. Sometimes it was his own, but sometimes it wasn't.

Lochlen took another step back, scanning the crowd, following the darkness until he saw him. Alek was sitting at a table shoved off to one side, twirling a finger around the rim of his glass. From the outside he looked completely composed, but that was how you could tell he was really agitated.

How many more times would he have to pull Alek from the edge only to watch him wander back?

Lochlen took a ragged breath. He needed a strategy. When Alek was like this, he followed one very strict rule: he never approached a soul. But anyone who made the first move was fair game, and in a room full of beer and testosterone, that could happen any second. *Fuck.* How did Lochlen always make it this far without a goddamn plan?

Lochlen scoured the walls, hoping to find a fire alarm to pull or an electrical panel to mess with, but even just standing alone in the crowd made him feel as if someone was constantly shouting in his ear. It was at times like this that he wished he could turn it off. He remembered asking his mom once what would happen if he removed the necklace for a while. That was when she revealed it was probably not a coincidence that the attack that killed his father occurred shortly after she'd passed down her crystal—that someone no doubt had been watching them for a while, that they'd waited to strike until the necklace was vulnerable. After that, she advised him to only ever take his necklace off if he was prepared to lose it.

So here he was, standing in a crowd of burly men, at a bar that stunk worse than a pirate ship, incapable of moving any closer to Alek and unable to think straight because of all the other emotions whirling around his head. And then, as fate would have it, he ran out of time.

He glanced back to see someone trip into Alek's table. *Don't do it.* He cast out the thought, hoping to command the pair of what looked like college freshman lingering at his friend's side. But unfortunately, his powers didn't work like that. The one who tripped made a big show of demanding an apology and when Alek didn't give him one, the second boy swiped whatever drink Alek had been nursing and held it up, ready to dump over his head. But before he even tilted the glass, a portly gentleman barreled past them, knocking the kid back and drenching his shirt in alcohol.

At the same time, someone breathed down Lochlen's neck and he squirmed, launching himself sideways. The second time it happened, he whirled to find everyone with their backs to him. The feeling persisted no matter where he moved, as if he were attempting to avoid his own shadow. *Someone was here.* But was it him they were after? Or was it—*Alek.* He whipped his head around again, reorienting himself in the crowd. Having lost sight of his friend, Lochlen pushed through the mass of bodies. When he caught sight of Alek again, he was standing instead of sitting, and Lochlen's stomach tightened. He knew exactly how this would end.

One second, all he could think was how fucking unfair this was, and the next, his mind was empty. Black. Save for three words: they deserved it.

Shit.

Lochlen bit down on his lip. He bit down as hard as he could, trying to stop himself from moving, because on the outside he was still in control, but on the inside . . . on the inside he wanted to smash every glass in this pub, just to hear them shatter. He wanted to find a knife and shred every goddamn leather stool, just to feel them tear. He wanted—no—he *needed* to destroy something. It was no longer a matter of *if.* It was a matter of *what.* Of *who.*

He bit down.

He wanted to hit someone.

He bit down.

He wanted to hurt someone.

He bit down.

He bit down.

He bit down.

But even as the metallic tang of blood coated his tongue, he couldn't stop himself from shoving through the crowd. He couldn't stop his feet from moving any more than he could stop his veins from constricting.

Next thing he knew, he was marching up to Alek's table. Next thing he knew, he was shoving someone's cheek against a wall of road signs and band flyers. Next thing he knew, he was telling Alek to sit the fuck back down or else.

Everything after that was a blur of fists being thrown and chairs being knocked over. It was a fit of ragged breaths and sharp grunts. It was a combination of sweat and beer dampening his hair as his head slammed into a table. And then it was a mix of blood and dirt encrusting his knuckles as he shot forward, his fist connecting with someone's jaw.

It was the slippery floors hindering his footwork, and the crowd around them parting and surging at random. It was a moment of foreboding as his eyes bounded the tavern in search of Alek. And then it was a flash of panic as someone grabbed him by the hood and pulled.

Then it was the lack of air in his lungs, the burning in his throat as he gasped between fits of coughing. It was the lights overhead spotting his vision and the ache in his skull reminding him he wasn't invincible. *Then*, it was his instincts telling him when to duck. It was Mirai's voice telling him not to waste his punches. It was adrenaline hurling him through the back door of the tavern.

Crack. He felt the sound in his teeth as he and a second body hit the pavement. And then again, as Lochlen's fist smashed into the guy's nose. Judging by the angle, he was pretty sure it was broken, but even that wasn't enough to make him stop. Lochlen hit the kid again, and again, and again. *And it still wasn't enough. It would never be enough.*

When his next breath was cold instead of hot, the air whipped through his lungs, and he shuddered. It felt as if he'd been underwater for a really long time and had finally broken through the surface.

Lochlen noticed the blood first. It was everywhere—all over the guy's mouth, on his shirt, staining Lochlen's hands, and splattering the pavement. He noticed the guy's face second because with his eyes shut and his hair swept back, he looked so much younger than Lochlen might've guessed. But it was the third thing he noticed that brought the entire world crashing down around him.

If Alek had looked like a shiny quarter, Aris was a goddamn diamond. She was a diamond in a crowd of beggars and pickpockets, and her fingers were curled around Alek's arm. Lochlen was both relieved and annoyed. At least now he understood why he'd suddenly felt more hungover than drunk, why the corners of his vision were no longer fuzzy, why he had someone pinned to the ground and no desire to keep swinging.

But when he processed what she must've just witnessed, Lochlen's entire body tensed. The expression scrawled across her face burned into his memory, and when someone dragged him back, slamming a foot into his chest, the pain was worse than anything he'd ever felt. Lochlen fell to his side, unable to breathe. His lungs were locked in place. The only air he could scrounge was whatever seeped through the cracks, and it felt like waiting for a dripping facet to fill a bathtub.

Did betraying a friend to save the world make him the villain or the hero? He was pretty sure he knew the answer now, because tonight, he'd done just the opposite. He'd come to save Alek and ended up with blood on his hands. And now, when Aris looked at him, it was fear in her eyes, not gratitude.

Once again, all he could think about was how fucking unfair this all was, but this time he didn't want to hurt anyone. He just wanted to go to sleep and not dream. He wanted to open his eyes and find Aris kneeling beside him. He wanted her to be as worried about him as she'd been about Alek. But instead, when Lochlen opened his eyes, Alek had a dazed expression and Aris still clung to his side.

When Lochlen finally drew himself to his feet, the guys were long gone, leaving the crowd in a frenzy. Some were laughing, others were trading cash, and a select few were butting heads, as if itching for a fight of their own. Lochlen moved to join his friends, flinching as Aris took a small step back. Alek moved with her, of course, which only made Lochlen want to keel over again, but instead he stopped dead in his tracks.

Villain.

Aris raised a finger. Her movements were stiff and Lochlen could have sworn she was holding her breath. He looked down to where she was pointing. One of his hands looked like it had gotten caught in a garbage compactor, all chewed up and crooked. It didn't hurt, but it probably would in the morning when his memory wasn't as fuzzy and the adrenaline in his veins wasn't working overtime to numb the pain. It was the same hand that Aris had grabbed that day at the shop. He continued to stare, knowing he would probably never hold her hand like that again. And not just because his fingers were broken, but because Alek's hand would be there for her instead, and his was indestructible.

Villain.

He slipped his other hand in front to hide his shame and then unclenched his teeth. "What are you doing here?" he said, but his voice was rough and his words came out like a growl.

Aris shrank. "I just wanted to make sure he was alright," she said, stumbling on a few of her words.

Lochlen glanced at Alek, who avoided his gaze. "Well, he looks pretty fucking alright to me." He flexed his good hand, unsure whether this was the last of Alek's anger escaping his system or his own flooding back. He sucked in a breath. *Of course she's here*, he thought. *Of course, she saw everything. And of course, Alek . . .* He reached up, grabbing the back of his neck as he glanced at the sky. Once again, Llewellyn was hidden behind a mask of clouds.

"We have to go," Lochlen breathed as a faint wail screeched in his ear. "Now."

The three of them dashed to Aris's car, but when Alek moved to leave with Lochlen, Aris's grip remained firm on Alek's arm. "I can take him," she said without meeting Lochlen's gaze.

Lochlen pressed his good hand to his forehead. They didn't have time for this. He opened his mouth to say something he would likely regret later, but Alek beat him to it. "I'll be fine," Alek told her. When Aris refused to release her grasp, he added "Just go" in a tone even harsher than Lochlen would have used.

Aris looked stricken. She said nothing more, just dropped his arm and climbed into her car, gravel crunching beneath her tires as she drove off.

Lochlen turned to Alek. He grabbed his friend's chin with his good hand and tilted it up, forcing Alek to look him in the eyes. "Great, you're pissed." Lochlen dropped his hand. "Give me your keys."

They both darted for the car and then sped off toward the alley, and sure enough, when Lochlen checked his mirror, the pub was buzzing with red and blue lights. He pressed a hand to his head as he pulled onto the main road and shifted his attention to Alek. "You know, you couldn't have picked a worse fucking time for this. I mean, for fuck's sake, if I hadn't—" He thought back to the feeling he'd gotten in the crowd, to whoever had been there, watching them. Was it the same person he'd sensed outside his window? The same person who'd riffled through Aris's locker? Lochlen slammed his hand against the dashboard, leaving a dark smear of blood. "You know, just because you're invincible doesn't mean the rest of us—"

Villain.

Seeing the way Alek sagged against the window, it was obvious he already knew all this. And he certainly didn't need Lochlen making him feel any worse about it.

It was useless dwelling on *what ifs*. What if Aris remembered him? What if she'd met him first? What if he hadn't tried so hard to push her away? The fact of the matter was, she'd come here tonight for Alek, which meant, despite whatever connection Lochlen had with her, she and Alek had one too.

He looked over at Alek, and then back down at his hand. "She really cares about you," Lochlen finally said in a faint voice. "Just . . . Just don't fuck it up." He flexed his grip on the steering wheel, and then let out a steely breath.

The car behind them honked as Lochlen swerved into the rightmost lane. He pulled into the parking lot of what claimed to be a twenty-four hour diner.

"Where are we going?" Alek asked, his voice stripped of emotion.

"To sober you up," Lochlen said, shoving the car into park. "There's something I need to tell you."

CHAPTER 32

"D on't touch that," Yuki yelped as Mirai snatched a book out from under his nose. Aris was still making her way into the kitchen when Yuki pushed up from the table in a fit.

"Where in the hell did you find this?" Mirai asked, flipping through nearly two hundred pages of Welsh prose.

"The library," he spat. "Now give it back."

Mirai twirled to evade his grasp, her eyes darkening. "We're supposed to stay away from there," she said pointedly.

"I know, I know." Yuki returned to his chair in a huff. "Even though it would significantly speed up my research," he added, projecting his voice toward the hall, to the room at the end, which Aris assumed belonged to his parents. Was it filled with boxes as well? The living room had been. The kitchen, while devoid of cardboard, did look awfully sparse. No coffee maker, no toaster, no drying rack. The only things left on the counter were a silver kettle and a roll of paper towels. Her stomach churned, and she thought again about telling her parents the truth. Alek had asked her not to, but maybe his invincibility was hindering his ability to see the severity of the situation. After all, someone had broken into the library. Seemed like an awful lot of trouble just to steal a research paper, which meant it probably wasn't just any research paper.

Aris turned to Yuki. "What was the subject of your mother's thesis?"

He folded his arms. "It was an analysis of historical inaccuracies in the Arthurian legends."

Her vision clouded a little as she tugged at the sleeve of her sweater, remembering what Alek said about Avalon and the hidden islands. It shouldn't have come as a surprise to learn the paper was related to their theories. After all, Yuki had been adamant about the thief being Anathemian. At the time, she'd chalked it up to paranoia more than anything, but now . . . She glanced over the barren countertops once more.

She still didn't want to believe the break-in was related to the shopkeeper. If anything, it sounded like the culprit was searching for Krysidia as well, but would that make them less dangerous than the reaper, or more? Aris tilted her head, her eyes falling back over Yuki. "Why would something like that need to be in the restricted section?"

"Well, she goes on to use those inaccuracies as evidence to suggest the story is more truth than legend." Aris opened her mouth again, but Yuki cut her off. "Whatever you're about to say, I've already considered it."

"Don't be an ass," Mirai said, thudding the back of his head.

Yuki whirled to face her, one hand buried in his stark-white hair. "You know, I was actually minding my business in here before you barged in and started stealing things."

Mirai pressed a finger to her lip and said, "Is stealing a stolen book really stealing though?" She waved it around by its cover, the pages flapping like the fringe at the bottom of a vintage dress.

Yuki raised both hands, eyebrows drawn together as if she were shaking a newborn child. His fingers curled at the sound of its spine cracking, and his eyes fell closed for a moment. "I refuse to apologize for being the only one who hasn't given up on Krysidia," he said through clenched teeth. "Now give it back."

Aris felt the hairs perk up on the back of Mirai's neck, and she wondered if Yuki knew how deep his words had cut. When Jada first mentioned Mirai trying to bring a katana into a coffee shop, Aris had assumed it meant she was freaked out enough to want to leave Elsley. But that wasn't the case at all. Jada had mentioned later that she'd been spending so much time at the dojo because she'd been trying to prove to her parents that she was capable of protecting them. She'd been trying to convince them to let her and Yuki finish the school year.

But of course, Mirai didn't say any of that to her brother. Instead, she raised the book above his head, threatening to tear one of the pages from its binding.

Yuki let out a strangled noise as he grabbed for her wrist, and in a flash, the two of them were halfway across the kitchen, words flying back and forth as he attempted to wriggle the book from her fingers. But if Mirai was using even an ounce of her strength, Aris imagined Yuki would have an easier time prying a piece of meat from the mouth of a greyhound.

Keeerrr. The edge of one of the earlier pages tore down the middle and Yuki let out a string of words, several of which weren't English. But whatever he said caused Mirai to falter long enough for him to peel back a few of her fingers, and a moment later the book came hurtling through the air.

Aris squeaked as it shot past her before landing face up, sliding beneath one of the chairs. Mirai moved to grab it, but Yuki held out an arm. "Wait," he said, the tension gone from his voice. "I want Aris to get it."

Mirai craned her head back to stare at him. "Uh, ew?"

Yuki rolled his eyes. "Do I even want to know what you're thinking?"

"Funny, I was about to ask you the same thing."

The two of them started bickering again, but it was softer this time, and for once, they looked more like friends than siblings. Aris wandered over to the table and crouched to retrieve the book. She dusted off the cover and flipped the whole thing over, studying the page beneath her thumb. At the top of the entry was a delicate illustration of a leafless tree. She traced one of its branches before handing it back to Yuki. He flipped the book shut and tucked it beneath his arm. He kept a finger nestled between the pages as a placeholder, and everything clicked—why he wanted her to be the one to pick it up. She'd read once that fortune tellers used to predict people's futures by interpreting a randomly selected book passage. Bibliomancy, it was called.

The more she thought about how desperately he tried to hide his intent, the more she wanted to laugh. After all, he was the same boy who'd asked her to start by keeping her mouth shut when she'd offered him her help at the library. In the end, her urge to laugh gave way to a subtle grin, because, just maybe, this meant he was starting to trust her.

"C'mon," Mirai said, tugging Aris's arm, "Jada probably thinks we've abandoned them."

Aris nodded, but as she turned to follow Mirai out through the dining room, she caught the slightest flicker of Yuki's gaze. His eyes rose to meet hers for the barest fragment of a second. It wasn't exactly a smile, but it made her feel as though eventually it could be.

She smirked at herself as she headed after Mirai, remembering the rush that came from feeling useful.

When they got to Mirai's room, Aris found Jada sitting on an island of terracotta sheets surrounded by a sea of clothes. Unlike in the living room, Mirai's boxes were all still untaped, leaning against the side of her dresser. "We're trying to decide what to wear for tomorrow's full moon," Jada explained. "You're coming, right?" Aris nodded as she folded up a pair of leggings, two sweaters, and a skirt before hunkering down beside them.

"Do you want to borrow something?" Mirai asked, throwing a black dress onto the bed. Jada picked it up, held it out next to Aris, then draped it over their own torso before tossing it aside.

Aris examined the baby doll silhouette strewn across the bed. "Are we meant to dress up?"

"Well, no one else ever does," Mirai said and then laughed. "At least, not that I can tell."

"Yuki dressed up that one time," Jada added as they picked through a pile of nearby scarves.

Mirai snorted. "Only because I put the rest of his clothes in the wash."

A pair of sandals came hurling through the air and Aris and Jada both ducked, Aris as if she were dodging a missile, and Jada as if it were a fistful of confetti they didn't feel like picking out of their hair.

"Speak of the devil," Mirai sighed, kicking a purse beneath her bed.

Yuki leaned against the door frame, eyes scanning the mess of clothes. "Mom told me to tell you that anything that's not packed by tomorrow morning is getting donated." Mirai threw a slipper at his head. Yuki batted it out of the way and scoffed. "Suit yourself," he called back as he continued down the hall.

"So have you heard from Alek?" Jada asked as Aris vigilantly raised her head. They turned to Mirai, adding, "He went AWOL last night."

"Again?" Mirai discarded the pair of earrings she was holding and began sifting through a small glass bowl for another.

Jada nodded. "And then, of course, Lochlen came home in a huff." They turned to Aris again, as if translating between the two. "That usually means he found him."

At that, Aris grabbed whatever she could reach and started folding. She didn't know why, but she was nervous to tell them the truth about following Lochlen. Something about the way Mirai had so casually said the word *again* made Aris's ribs squeeze together. Because to her, last night had felt like the end of the world, and now Mirai was brushing it off as if it were a minor annoyance.

"For fuck's sake." Mirai pressed the backs of her hands to her eyes. "You know what? Whatever," she snapped, dragging her fingers down either side of her face. "He just better not be grumpy for the full moon tomorrow." She leaned against the wall, stepping into a single heeled shoe, and then, with a purse of her lips, she kicked it off.

Maybe it wasn't as bad as Aris thought. Maybe Lochlen didn't normally go around breaking people's noses. Maybe last night was a fluke. Maybe he'd been in the wrong place at the wrong time. Maybe it was self-defense. Maybe, maybe, maybe, she thought, the words echoing in her mind like, *please, please, please.*

"So this kind of thing happens a lot?" Aris asked, bunching up a pair of tights.

Mirai answered, "Yes" at the same time Jada said, "No." They exchanged a glance. Mirai grabbed a jacket from the middle of the pile that Aris had just finished folding, destroying the rest of the tower in the process. She held it up in front of the mirror and then added it to a stack on her dresser that Aris could only assume was a "maybe" pile. "It's kind of like having a werewolf as a best friend," Mirai explained. "Most of the time he's fine, but once in a while he turns into a raging monster and you kind of just have to chain him to a wall and hope he doesn't kill anyone."

"That," Jada started, tilting their head to ponder, "is actually not a bad analogy."

Mirai jumped onto the bed, landing in a scatter of cardigans and knee socks. "I know, right? I was watching this god-awful teen drama, and suddenly it hit me. He basically has the charm of a vampire with the temperament of a werewolf."

Jada broke into a grin and the two of them fed off each other's amusement until they both toppled over, faces pressed into pillows.

Mirai lifted her head. "Remember that time?"

Jada threw a hand over their mouth and nodded. "With the handcuffs?"

If Aris wasn't a prophet, she might not have discerned the remorse lacing their breath, or the somberness in their eyes, the way their laughter masked the fear they both felt. Suddenly, the word *again* felt heavier.

She knew then that last night hadn't been a fluke, that Lochlen hadn't been in the wrong place at the wrong time. He simply was not the boy she thought he was—the boy she *hoped* he was.

Mirai curled over, clutching her stomach. "I really thought Alek was going to murder us all right then."

Aris froze. "You mean Lochlen," she said, her voice rippling as a sweater slipped through her fingers, landing in a rumpled heap on the floor.

"No, I mean Alek." Mirai pulled a leather stiletto out from under her and chucked it to the side.

"It's just . . . well, Lochlen was the one who . . . I thought—" She didn't know what she thought, except that seeing Lochlen last night had scared her. It scared her the way the hairbrush scared her, the way seeing her dream-self with a gun scared her.

"Lochlen just doesn't know when to give up," Mirai clarified. "Yuki thinks he's got a savior complex, but sometimes I wonder if he's gotten a little too addicted to the chaos."

Aris frowned down at a demolished pile of clothes, replaying the conversation over in her head, this time with Alek as the werewolf/vampire. It made even less sense than it had the first time. A trickle of relief flowed through her as she realized she'd been wrong about Lochlen—or rather, right about him. But it was quickly drowned out by the dark cloud that was Alek. Alek, who'd never stepped on a flower. Alek, who'd shown up at her school and dazzled her history teacher with his knowledge of ancient technology. Alek, who'd driven her through the mountains just to watch a thunderstorm. Alek, who'd spent his life chasing a legend in order to protect his friends. *Alek, who'd nearly kissed her in his grandfather's parlor.*

It didn't feel real. It didn't seem possible that Alek could have a whole different side to him. That *he* had not been the boy she thought he was. Aris needed a distraction. She needed something to do with her hands that wasn't refolding the same pair of leggings for the zillionth time. She wished she had her sketchbook with her, but she settled for an old index card she sometimes used as a bookmark. "Maybe I shouldn't come tomorrow," she said, letting a pencil drag blindly across the paper.

Mirai leaped off the bed. "What? No, you have to." She and Jada both looked at each other, then at the floor. In a feeble voice, she said, "It's our last full moon together."

Nothing about what Mirai said suggested it was Aris's fault, and yet, she couldn't help but feel responsible. Maybe if she hadn't gone to that party, if she hadn't met Alek, if she hadn't learned the truth about her ring, maybe then tomorrow would be just another full moon. Not their last. *Not her first.*

It didn't seem fair. Before meeting Alek, Aris had lived each day as if crossing them off on a calendar. She'd spent her life always waiting for something to happen, and now that it had, time seemed to be the only thing missing. It felt as if she'd made a deal with a demon or the devil or a god, like they'd granted her the life she'd always wanted in exchange for her soul—the catch being she had only thirty days to live it. But she understood now why book characters were always making those kinds of deals—thirty days with these people and their magic and their castle in the woods were worth trading a lifetime without.

Mirai turned to Jada. "Have you made a decision, by the way?"

"Not exactly . . ."

"My parents offered to take Jada with us when we go," Mirai explained. "But they're totally in love with Lochlen's brother and—"

"Mirai!" Jada hurled a pair of socks at her, but she swatted them back. They ricocheted off the side of their shoulder and Mirai smirked arrogantly. "Well fine," Jada drawled. "If we're gonna talk about crushes, maybe we should start with—" Mirai leaped onto the bed, one hand firmly pressed to Jada's mouth as she tackled them into a heap of pillows.

There was a string of muffled words that Aris couldn't make out, and then there was dead silence as Mirai's eyes burned their way into Jada's soul. When she finally released her grip on them, she bounced up from the bed and strolled toward the closet as if nothing had happened. "So, Aris," she said teasingly, "if you had to pick, which, uh, *shoes* do you like better? The brown boots or the taupe knee highs?" She held up one of each, raising the taupe one slightly higher as she waited for Aris to choose.

But Jada, whose head was still nestled between two pillows, erupted into laughter. "Do not answer that," they said to Aris between breaths.

Mirai frowned, and both shoes hit the ground with a soft thud. Aris pressed her lips together and wiggled a brow. She leaned over, trying to discern what was wrong with the shoes and why Jada hadn't wanted her to pick one. "I'm not even going to ask," she started to say when she saw a pair of all-black sneakers poking out from beneath the bed.

When she sensed Jada's eyes following her own, she veered her gaze, refocusing on the drawing in front of her. The lines were rough, but there was no doubting the resemblance. It was the tree she'd seen in Yuki's book, the page she'd turned to by what she now knew was no coincidence. It was not unlike the one she'd seen in the mountains. She remembered the feeling she'd gotten in her stomach. She thought about that tree blocking the road and how it had forced them to take a different route. Maybe she was meant to drive past it. Just like she was meant to end up at the library. Everything felt like a sign and they were all pointing toward one thing: Yuki's book. But there was something still bothering her about the image. Like there was another clue. Something she was forgetting.

She closed her eyes, trying to picture it. There was a memory there, and she drilled into it, but the image was slipping away. She reached as if to grab it, but the most she got was a wall of stone and then—her mind cut to an image of a bloodied hand dangling limply at someone's side. Aris's eyes shot open.

She thought of Lochlen. Only this time, he was younger. This time, he was surrounded by blue hydrangeas.

Aris turned to Jada again, her voice laced with sympathy. "How's his hand?"

"I'm pretty sure it's broken." They'd known right away she was talking about Lochlen. They sighed. "Not that he would let me close enough to see it, let alone heal him." Jada met her gaze. "But how did you—"

Mirai's squeal snatched both their attention as she hauled a dress from the depths of her closet. She bounded across the room, draping the fabric over Aris's torso with a smirk.

Aris stared down at the gold flowers adorning a corset top. "I don't know if it's really my style."

"Aris, this dress was made for you," Mirai protested. "It's not even my size."

Aris shook off a lopsided grin. "Why did you buy it then?"

"I don't remember, okay, but as of this moment, I'm convinced it was so you could wear it to your first full moon at the ruins." She bounced on the balls of her feet in a cute half dance. "C'mon, Aris, it's fate."

Aris let out a sigh, trying to resist Mirai's contagious grin. Finally, she held out a hand. "Who am I to dispute the stars?" she said with a smirk and then slipped the sleeves from the hanger.

CHAPTER 33

A lek woke up in a haze that morning, the taste of regret thick on his tongue, though that could've been the rum. It was hard to tell. His temple ached, or at least he thought it did. Maybe Lochlen had just complained of the pain so many times that Alek had convinced himself he knew the feeling.

Sometimes, he stayed up late trying to remember what things were like before he had received his ring. When he first met Aris, he told her he'd never been injured. It wasn't exactly a lie, but it couldn't have been the truth either, because for the nine years before his ring, he'd been just as helpless as the rest of the world. The problem was, if he had been injured, he couldn't remember it, no matter how much he wanted to. It was a stupid curiosity, Alek knew that. But if pain was part of what made people human, maybe its absence was what made him feel most like a monster. Maybe that was why, no matter how many mornings he woke up with his stomach in knots, it was never enough to break the cycle. Guilt wasn't the same as empathy. The dullness in his chest wasn't the same as having your nose bashed into your face or the air kicked from your lungs.

Alek fought the urge to run back to his car and drive deep into the forest. Maybe if he closed his eyes beneath an oak tree, its wisdom might purge his shame. He usually kept to himself the morning after and sometimes for a couple days, but in this case that wasn't an option. He couldn't continue avoiding Aris and expect her to forgive him. Lochlen had known that too. So here Alek was, sitting on her front porch, a coffee in either hand, trying not to lose his nerve before she got home.

The worst part of Aris showing up last night wasn't even the fact that she'd found him at that sleazy bar. It was the guilt he'd felt when he saw her small frame push through the crowd. Anything could have happened to her. *Anything*. And it would have been his fault. Sometimes Alek wished he could project his power onto others, or even transfer it completely. And never so much as in that moment. The twenty meters away she'd been from him . . . the forty seconds it'd taken to get to her . . . he'd never asked his god for a favor before. But last night, he did. And Alek was still awaiting its price. Although a part of him thought maybe Lochlen had already paid it.

Alek frowned down at the paper cups in his hands. They no longer felt warm. He had been sitting in front of her house for the better half of an hour, and today had been colder than normal. Fall was definitely here.

The sound of a car door slamming sent Alek jumping to his feet, and if it weren't for his ring, he certainly would have spilled one of the drinks. His hands were trembling so badly it couldn't have been anything less than Lady Luck herself holding on to them.

"Alek?" Aris's voice almost got lost in the wind. The gust tugged at her sweater and played with her hair, but even with the elements against her, she looked as beautiful as ever.

"I brought you coffee," Alek rushed to say. "But it's cold now, I think. Um, we could go get new ones? I mean, if you want." God, this was pathetic. He'd had all day to rehearse and still managed to trip over his own tongue.

"It's okay," Aris said, accepting the drink from him anyway. "It's getting kind of late."

Alek clutched the cup in his hand. Of course she didn't want coffee. He should've brought tea, or hot chocolate maybe?

"So, did you come to tell me what you were doing at that dive bar?" Aris asked.

Yes. *No.* Alek dragged a foot, tracing a half circle around a stray leaf that had blown up from the lawn. "I, uh . . . I went there for a drink."

Her expression dampened. "Your grandfather doesn't have enough of those in his parlor?"

Alek raked his free hand through his hair and said, "I guess not."

They were walking now, both still holding the coffees that neither one of them planned to drink. The paper cups felt like a wall between them, something preventing either of them from reaching out to the other, and when Alek took a deep breath and said, "Look, I never wanted you to see that side of me," it felt as if the words smacked into that wall and died.

Aris took a hurried step, just enough to put them out of sync with each other, to put her a half pace ahead of him. "Is that supposed to be an apology? Because it sucks."

His saliva felt thick and sticky in his mouth. "I'm sorry, I'm just . . ." He slowed his pace so it matched the rhythm of the words as they fell out of his mouth. "I'm just trying to protect you."

She turned back, shoulders hunched forward as if the cup in her hands was made of lead instead of paper. "And I'm just trying to understand you. Because I don't see how disappearing like that protects anyone."

Alek raised a brow. "Are you saying you wouldn't have tried to stop me?"

A pause, and then Aris looked away. She started walking again and this time Alek hastened to keep up. "I'm saying that even if I had, at least I would've known what I was walking into. I'm saying that between the shopkeeper and the library, and what happened with your grandfather, I would've been relieved to know you hadn't been kidnapped. I'm saying you could've at least sent me a text to let me know you weren't dead."

Alek stroked the side of his neck. "My phone sort of ran out of battery," he said, regretting the words as he spoke them.

Aris whirled. "I don't care if your phone had been run over by a truck and then chucked into the ocean. If you had wanted me to know you were safe, you would've found a way." She marched across the street, throwing open the gate to a tiny cemetery at the edge of the woods. He made it as far as the fence and stalled. Alek had been lectured before, several times. But even though the last girl who'd scolded him could literally snap a piece of steel with her fingers, hearing this from Aris was scarier.

It was the strings again, he realized as he inched past a tombstone barely visible beneath a thick layer of moss. The fragile threads he'd been so worried would break. And yet here was Aris, no more than twenty feet away, and somehow their connection felt thinner than ever. Their bond had diminished to a single strand of silk, and when Alek spoke, it felt as if he were tiptoeing across it. "It's not that I . . ." he started, and then lost his balance. "I just . . ." Alek raked a hand through his hair and tried again. "Sometimes I get in these moods, and it's like everything else is blocked out. I end up fixated on one thought and it plays over and over in my head and the more I try to reason it out, the less sense it makes. And then I just get so mad that I . . ."

So close. He'd been so close.

But now Aris was looking at him like he'd just sprouted a pair of fangs. "Alek, why were you at that bar?"

He tapped a foot against the edge of a tombstone. "You know, Lochlen knew exactly what he was walking into, and you saw how that turned out."

"Yeah, well, fighting's not really my thing." Aris shrugged, and then wandered to one of the benches.

"I don't think it's his either."

Her voice thickened. "Does it always end up like that?"

"No." Alek took an uneven breath. "Sometimes Lochlen loses." He thought back to how many times he'd forced Lochlen to let Jada heal him, how many times Lochlen had locked Alek to streetlights, or drainpipes, or trees, just to keep him from winning a fight.

"So you went there to fight?" Alek nodded as Aris pulled her knees up against her chest. "But your powers, won't they—" Alek nodded again.

He stuffed his hands in his pockets, glancing up toward the sky. The moon was out there somewhere, judging him, no doubt. "Every time it happens, I wake up the next morning and vow never to do it again, but—"

"But what? Alek . . . you could seriously hurt someone." She lowered her voice to a whisper. "You could *kill* someone. I mean, Brent barely touched you that night and you nearly took down the whole barn."

Alek ambled through the tombstones and sat on the other end of the bench. "Don't you think I know that?" he said, choking out the words.

"So what? You just don't care?"

Alek was quiet for a long time, and when Aris moved to tuck a piece of hair behind her ear, he noticed a thin red scab down the length of her palm. His voice turned to ice. "Did that happen last night?" he uttered, gesturing at her hand.

"No, uh, Jada . . ." Aris remained perfectly still as she blinked, like a deer lost in a flood of headlights. "We went to a park," she explained, forcing a smile. "I guess it didn't like me very much."

Alek chose a spot on the other side of the graveyard to stare at. A runt of a tree. It had just a handful of red leaves on its delicate branches. "Have you ever lit something on fire?" Alek asked, setting his cup down on the armrest. "Accidentally, I mean."

Leaning forward, Aris nodded. "My dad's research notes."

Alek made a face like he'd just said the word *yikes*, and then continued. "Was your first thought whether to extinguish the flames, or was it *how* to extinguish them?"

"How." She said the word the way a person might answer a math question, with the pointedness of knowing there was only one correct answer.

Alek stared down at his boots. The mud had clung to them where the ground remained damp beneath the leaves. He paddled his feet gently to unstick them. "That's kind of what it feels like. Sometimes I get so mad that it's no longer a question of whether I destroy something. It's *how*. It's *what*." He paused. "It's *who*. That's why I avoid everyone, and that's why I ended up at that bar. I can't stand the thought of hurting someone I care about."

"You don't really think you would . . ."

Alek leaned back and said, "How'd you end up putting the fire out?"

"Uh," Aris replied, clearly scrambling to recall. "Evie's unicorn housecoat." Alek gave her a look and Aris rushed to explain herself. "I just grabbed whatever was closest . . ." Alek could see the moment she figured it out. Her mouth hung open and her gaze faltered.

Alek's voice was the slow gritty texture of burnt sugar as he said, "When I'm like that, the last thing I want is for *you* to be what's closest."

Aris picked at the paper liner on her cup. "What happened after you dropped me off the other day?"

"Nothing. Stephen just gave me a bunch of chores to do." Alek shook his head.

"Then why were you so scared when you heard him come home?" she pressed.

He didn't want to tell her the truth, because the truth sounded too much like an excuse. He didn't want to tell her because he didn't want her to look at him the way Mirai sometimes did when she thought he

381

wasn't looking. He didn't want to tell her because he didn't want to guilt her into staying. But he knew none of that was going to stop him. Because for the hundred times Stephen had made Alek want to remove his ring, he remembered that the only time he'd actually taken it off had been for Aris. He'd only just met her then, and yet the thought of losing her had made him so frantic that he'd done the one thing he'd been warned never to do. The feeling he had now was the same, but amplified. Before, it was just in his chest, but now it was everywhere—in the hand she'd grabbed that day in the mountains, in the leg she'd brushed when she bent down to fix his laces. It was jittery fingers and wings fluttering in his stomach, and the memory of her eyes sparkling when she first saw the ruins. It was the giddiness he'd felt upon learning he'd been right, that she was one of them.

Alek turned in his seat to face her. "Did you notice the cut on Stephen's cheek?" Aris nodded. "The other day, he caught me adjusting the mileage on his Ambassador." Alek thrummed his fingers against the bench, staring at the ground again. "At first he just yelled a lot, but then it escalated and he ended up hurling a scotch glass at me. Of course, it didn't hit me. Instead, it hit the edge of the table and one of the shards bounced back and nicked his cheek."

He slowly raised his eyes.

"I think I was eight when Stephen first told me my mother was dead. At least, I thought that's what he'd said, but apparently *dead* and *dead to us* are two very different things. But it wasn't until I turned thirteen that he started drinking a lot. He often revealed bits and pieces about my parents, but it took a while to put it all together. They were only seventeen when they had me, and Stephen arranged to take custody so my mom could go off to school like they'd always planned. Once she graduated, he figured she would come back and work part time for his firm. He thought she would be old enough at that point to do the whole mom thing. But I guess without any legal obligation to care for me, she took a job at some high-end tech company overseas."

Alek curled and uncurled his fingers, hoping the motion would distract him from thinking too deeply. He wanted to be able to say the words without feeling them. To explain without drowning in contemplation. He took a deep breath and said, "Sometimes it feels like I can't even be mad at him, because he did what he thought was best and got screwed over for it."

Aris jolted forward, hands gripping her knees. "Just because things didn't go the way he planned, doesn't make it okay to try and hurt . . . someone." The words died on her tongue, and Alek watched her fingers limply slide down her legs.

"Ironic, isn't it?" he said. "Stephen hates me for reminding him of my father—when it's *him* I ended up most like. Though, in a way, I might even be worse. At least when Stephen chucks his scotch glass, he knows it'll never actually hit me."

"Wait, he knows?"

"Not about my ring or anything, but you can only miss a target so many times before you suspect the game is rigged."

"But then, why would he—"

"Because he knows it's my fault. And he knows I know it, too. So he pushes. He lets my powers batter him until I do what I'm told, or I beg for his forgiveness, or I promise to earn his approval." Aris had one hand over her mouth, and he recognized the expression in her eyes. It was the same look she had after touching her parents' license plate.

"Come with me," she said in a weak voice.

"You don't understand. Stephen's not just going to let me go. My mom doesn't want his money, and she doesn't need his firm. I'm the only bargaining chip he's got left. He still thinks he'll be able to lure her back."

Aris scooted along the bench until their knees were nearly touching. "What if we found your dad?"

Alek dropped his head into his hands. "I've tried. Not even Lochlen could figure out where he lives." He sucked in a breath as he straightened. "Look, it's fine. I'm fine," he assured. "In nine months, I'll be eighteen. Then there's nothing he can do to keep me here."

Aris wrapped her arms around her sides. "If you were fine, you wouldn't have gone to that bar last night."

He grinned lazily, if only because it was easier than frowning. Then he bobbed his head and said, "Yeah, okay, fair point."

Aris's mouth dropped open, and for a second Alek thought she was about to scold him again, but instead, her head tilted a couple degrees to the left and her lips fell back together. They curved as they landed. She was smiling at him, finally, and a weight lifted off Alek's chest. A hint of pink kissed her cheeks when she noticed him staring. "I'm going to find Krysidia," she offered.

"What?"

"I'm going to find Krysidia," she repeated, although this time it sounded more like a promise than a question.

Chapter 34

Aris must've been studying faerie legends. The sketchbook Garret had taken from her locker was full of them. Harrison had read the same Celtic tales as a boy. The similarities between Krysidians and the supernatural race that disappeared from Ireland some two thousand years ago were too seamless to be a coincidence, and most of what he'd read of the Arthurian legends only went to further that theory. Harrison had nearly laughed when he'd first seen her drawings. The likenesses between legends didn't extend to facial features like pointed ears and vampire fangs, and he'd certainly never met an Anathemian with wings, but Harrison could read between the lines.

It wasn't just her and Aleksander. There were five of them—six if she'd included her sister. He'd made note of the katana in one of the drawings and what looked like a history book in the other. Anathemians were supposed to be rare, but somehow, *six* of them had found each other.

Harrison thought about something Braxton used to say, that Elsley was like a waterfall. The phrase had completely gone over his head as a child, but now he understood it perfectly. Elsley was a constant stream of Anathemians, ripe for the picking if you knew how to spot them. And Brax definitely knew.

A cat nuzzled up against Harrison's leg, but this time he didn't sneeze. This time he'd arrived at the café with a bloodstream full of antihistamines. He hated looking so vulnerable, so pathetic. With his ring, Brax could probably take down an entire army and live to tell the tale. Meanwhile Harrison was debilitated by a few feline skin particles.

"So, let's hear it," Brax said as if he were an investor waiting for a return and Harrison had yet to prove his worth.

Harrison's stomach wrenched, but he managed a nod, painfully aware that he was a mouse in a room full of cats. Picking at a loose thread on his jacket, he began listing things off at random: Aris's class schedule, her favorite coffee shop, the license plate of the matte black car that had been picking her up and dropping her off at school. He answered a series of questions, dancing around the specifications of her powers—the one thing Garret hadn't been able to determine—and when Brax seemed to catch on to that fact, Harrison revealed the ruined cathedral Garret had discovered while following her through the woods. At that, Brax's interest seemed to pique.

"And the boy?" Brax asked, his disdain returning.

Harrison hesitated, fingers digging into his thighs. This was what he wanted, what he'd dreamed of, and all he had to do was lead Brax to the ring. The problem was, Harrison couldn't stop thinking about what would happen next. Brax didn't know who Aleksander was, couldn't know.

Harrison attempted to form his lips around the words, to say something about the kid's powers or his routine, but the answers all got stuck in his throat. When the words refused to come out, he tried to swallow them down. But the lump didn't budge.

Brax reached for his pocket, and Harrison was so sure he was going to pull out a knife that he squeezed his eyes shut. But the sound of something skittering across the table steadied his breathing. It wasn't a knife. It was a pen.

"Your brother gave me that." Braxton's voice was soft with affection. "He said I had too many wild ideas and suggested I write them down. He always thought I'd become an author someday." Harrison turned it over in his hand. An engraving caught the light and the word *dreamer* flashed up at him. *Elias must've picked this out long before Aleksander was born.* "Elias would be proud of you, you know," Brax continued. "I'm sure it didn't always seem like it, but he loved you more than anyone." Harrison made to hand it back, but Brax held up his hand. "You keep it," he said. "After all, you're the dreamer now."

Braxton's smile could melt a boy's heart, and yet Harrison didn't blush. All he could think about now was Elias, and the picture frame he'd found in his desk: "World's Greatest Uncle." More like world's *worst* uncle.

The room was warmer now than it had been, and it didn't help that the familiar orange cat had flopped down across his feet. He needed to get out of here.

"I need more time." Harrison choked out the words.

Brax's expression soured. "That's not what we agreed."

Harrison avoided his gaze, his eyes shooting to an armchair at the back of the room. The hairs on the back of his neck electrified when the man sitting lazily with a book in his hand glanced up, like he had felt Harrison looking. His bright red hair was pulled into a knot on the top of his head, and from this distance Harrison noticed a scar running horizontally across his pale face. It disconnected on either side of his nose before continuing along both cheeks. The man bared his teeth and Harrison nearly jumped back in his chair.

"There are five of them," Harrison exclaimed, the words shooting out of his mouth before he could think them through.

Brax crossed his arms, shoulders hunched over the table, but his gaze remained questioning and Harrison resisted the urge to bite his lip. He'd fucked up, he realized, as the corner of Braxton's mouth quirked. He'd fucked up so badly that part of him wished it had been a knife in Brax's pocket after all. It was a very small part, but the thought was there.

Harrison opened his mouth. Maybe it wasn't too late, maybe he could fix this. But before he could get a word out, Brax said, "I'll send someone after the girl in the next couple of days. Can I expect info on the others by next week?"

"You can't!" Brax stroked his chin, his patience clearly running low. "They're all friends," Harrison rushed to say. "So going after one might tip off the rest."

Brax leaned forward, his jaw set, his gaze boring into Harrison's skull. And then— "Five days."

Harrison nodded furiously as he slid out of his chair. The cat swatted at his leg as if to punish him for disrupting its nap, but then followed him benignly down the stairs.

The sun had long since set by the time he left. Most of the shops had turned off their lights for the night and only a handful of the streetlamps worked. Harrison trudged through the dark, breathing a sigh of relief when he finally arrived at his car. He had no idea what to do next, but at least he'd gotten out of there in one piece.

He fumbled for his keys and was reaching for the door when a massive gust of wind tore through the laneway. He was still tugging on the handle when something knocked him back. A flash of red hair. Harrison opened his mouth to scream, but the air was subsequently sucked from his lungs.

There were three of them, but even one would've been enough to frighten him. "The cathedral." The redhead glowered. "Where is it?"

The air flooded back to his chest and Harrison gasped. "I-I don't know."

And then the air was gone again. He dropped to the ground, watching the man's fingers curl and uncurl as if he were manipulating the air itself. It was excruciating, like being battered by waves. The man would let him thrash his way to the surface and then hurl him back under.

It didn't take long for Harrison to give up the location. The man had stood there, his hand curled into a fist as Harrison's head threatened to explode, and when he finally gave him his breath back, Harrison had screamed the coordinates into the night.

There was no one else around. No one to hear him. *No one to save him.*

The cement was cold against his cheek and as he heaved onto the pavement, he prayed that the worst of it was over. But Llewellyn never seemed to listen.

He understood now that the other two probably hadn't been ordered to come, that they'd likely volunteered. The redhead finally stepped back, and the other two moved in. They kicked him like he was a piece of trash on the side of the road, like he was every person they'd ever hated, every job they never got, every date that never called. Harrison thought his body would eventually go numb, but it didn't; he felt every blow, the one to his stomach, the one to his nose. He brought his arms up to shield his face, but they ached as he moved them, like pins were stabbing his skin from the inside.

"You really think this spineless piece of shit found five Anathemians?" asked one of the men between kicks.

"No," the redhead answered. "I think he found six."

Harrison's blood ran cold.

The redhead crouched, his mouth low against Harrison's ear. "You really think Brax doesn't know about your skryer?" he said, his voice a low slither. Harrison jerked, lashing out with all he had—which, apparently, was a weak swipe of a half-curled fist. The redhead didn't even bother to dodge. "Hurry up," he said with a smirk. "We have lambs to slaughter."

The last thing Harrison remembered was his own scream as a boot came down on his fingers, grinding them against the pavement, and then all three of them took off running.

He took a shaky breath as he lay crooked, a dark scuff on the dimly lit street. When he was sure they were really gone, he finally let himself cry.

He cried because his ribs ached and his back felt raw. He cried because his left foot was going numb and his nose was definitely broken. He cried because Brax had never truly cared for him and he never would. But most of all, he cried because, in a moment of hesitation, his conscience had gone and ruined everything.

He wiped his face with his sleeve, the action turning his once-gray sweater into a mess of purple splotches as it absorbed his own blood. He caught sight of his crumpled hand. At least two of his fingers were broken, but right now, all he could think about was his ring. The ring that was supposed to protect him from exactly this moment. A ring that would end up in the hands of the highest bidder.

He'd been stupid to hunt Brax down, to think he could trust him. He was stupid, *period*.

For a moment he thought he might die there, all alone in the street, but it was a long moment, and somewhere in it he dreamed up exactly what he intended to do if he survived. Harrison laid there in a puddle of his own blood, with his chest on fire and unable to breathe through his nose. And as he did, he stared up at the moon, at Llewellyn, making her both a promise and a threat.

CHAPTER 35

The air wasn't warm enough to be wearing a dress, but when Aris reached for her sweater, Mirai stole it from her hand and locked it in the trunk. "Now that's dealt with." She brushed her hands together. "You ready?"

Aris shivered. Something felt off about the woods tonight, as if the trees were larger than usual, heavier. Her body seemed to crumple under the sheer weight of their presence, and she couldn't help but remember the pocket watch she'd found at the antique shop, and how it'd had a similar effect. "Are you sure it's safe for us to be here? I mean, if it's Anathemians who are after us, doesn't that make the ruins the worst place to be?"

"Lochlen would've told us if it wasn't."

Aris might've argued if it wasn't for the katana strapped to Mirai's back. Instead, she tugged at the gold hem falling loosely over her knees, wishing she'd worn thicker tights. "I feel kind of—"

"Majestic? I know, right? Alek's going to lose his mind." Mirai looped a hand through Aris's arm, making her oddly nostalgic for the day they first met, which seemed silly because nostalgia was supposed to be reserved for years long since passed, and that first day had been barely two weeks ago. But to Aris, those couple of weeks had been like climbing a mountain. It didn't matter how few horizontal miles she'd covered, because it was the vertical ones that mattered. And as she and Mirai made their way through the dimly lit woods, as Aris tapped a finger against one of the mauve floral appliqués adorning her torso, and as Mirai's anticipation billowed through the surrounding air, Aris knew the view from the top had been well worth the climb.

Small flames dancing in the windows. That was the first thing she saw. Their castle smelled of sage and old books, and as the two of them slipped beneath the stone archway, they found pillows jumbled in the far corner and blankets draped like tablecloths over the larger pieces of debris. Yuki was leaning against a turquoise cushion, a crisp white collar peeking out from his oversized shirt, and a bottle in his hand instead of a book. Seeing him without a book gave Aris the same sensation as seeing her father without his glasses.

Mirai released her arm as Jada whisked past them, the hem of a lilac linen dress dragging against the tile as they made their way from corner to corner, a stick of smoldering sage in their hand. Lochlen had a bundle as well, and though his back was turned, Aris could see him wafting it over his tarot deck as Mirai dug her claws into his arm.

It should've been weird: seeing Mirai in her burgundy satin gown standing beside Lochlen, who was dressed as always. Same black hoodie. Same black jeans. Same black sneakers. And yet, it wasn't. Because this was their castle. *Their* family. *Their night.*

He turned then and Aris noticed his necklace was tucked away, leaving his eyes the only shred of color. Eyes that looked paler when he saw her, colder. Mirai leaned up to whisper something in his ear and for a split second, the gloomy boy went rigid. For a split second, Aris could've sworn she saw him blush. But then his features reset. He tucked his deck into his pocket. He passed his stick of sage to Mirai. And he darted for the window.

Aris had her lip between her teeth, fighting the urge to follow him—

"You look nice," a voice said, startling her. Aris spun to find Alek leaning against the wall, smiling.

"It's Mirai's," she rushed to say, touching a hand to her neck. Suddenly all she could think was that Mirai had been right, Alek really did look good in everything. His outfit, consisting of a black sweater and a rust-colored jacket, was similar to one she'd seen before, and yet, there was something different about him tonight. It was the ruins. The stars. The trees. The stone. *This* was his home.

At first, it was just the two of them. Alek, staring at her with his sparkly eyes, and Aris, realizing how quickly the space between them had narrowed. But before she could close the gap entirely, Mirai came gallivanting through the archway, a crown of woven branches in her hand. She placed it atop Aris's head, dubbing her queen, and whisked her off to the center of the ruins, twirling her in circles until they collapsed in a dizzy tangle of limbs.

Then it was Jada offering Aris a sip of elderflower wine as the sun's last breath gave way to night, and the four of them stared up at the stars. It was Mirai's head in Jada's lap as she told Aris about their first full moon together. It was the tightness with which Jada held Mirai's hand, and the single tear rolling down Mirai's cheek even as she laughed.

Then they were up. She and Alek. Jada and Mirai. They were ambling through the woods, guided by moonlight. They were scavenging for rocks, and flowers, and herbs. They were selecting the prettiest ones to bring to Llewellyn.

Then it was the four of them flooding the steps of the crypt. It was Alek and Aris and Mirai, all halting in unison as they saw Yuki kneeling in front of Llewellyn's altar, playing a wooden flute. It was the breath Aris held, waiting for his song to finish, and Yuki's ears turning bright red upon perceiving his audience.

Then it was the five of them silently praying. It was Jada from the top of the stairs, and the rest of them at the foot of Llewellyn's portrait. It was knowing, despite her powers, that all five of them were asking for the same thing. *Krysidia.*

And then, as Aris ascended the steps, it was the quiet, hollow feeling in her chest. It was seeing Lochlen perched atop the window, his feet hanging dangerously close to a grouping of tea lights. It was his absence from everything, and the metal door slamming shut whenever she glanced his way.

She didn't think. She hauled herself from the windowsill to the arch, nearly lighting her boots on fire as she kicked off from the stone. After fixing the skirt of her dress and brushing the loose curl from her eyes, she expected Lochlen to look up at her. Instead, he was staring at her boots as they dangled beside his shins.

When a laugh escaped his lips, Aris dropped her gaze, worried her boots really were on fire. But Lochlen simply muttered, "Forget-me-nots" and shook off a placid grin. Aris tapped her toes together, examining the now-dried blue flowers still woven between her laces. She waited for him to elaborate, but all he said was, "Anything missing from your locker?"

Her legs went limp. "My sketchbook," she said, trying to swallow the bout of nerves welling in her throat. "That and my math homework," she added with forced levity. "Though I'm pretty sure that one's my fault."

Lochlen touched a finger to his brow. At least his hand looked better. He must've finally let Jada heal it. Although, maybe that was more for Alek's sake than his own. "Drawn anything—interesting, lately?" he said in a stiff voice.

Aris was glad for the cold then, for the air that nipped at her cheeks, turning them a permanent shade of pink. "Actually"—her toes perked up again—"I drew us."

"Us?"

"The six of us, I mean. Actually, just the five of you—or four." She never did get around to finishing. "I would've drawn you next," she rushed to say, "but then it was lunch and, well, you already know the rest."

Lochlen gave a slow nod.

"Sorry," Aris murmured, tucking a piece of hair behind her ear.

"For what?"

"Not drawing you." She traced the petals of a mauve rose embroidered on her sleeve. "I don't want you to think it was on purpose or anything."

Lochlen stared at her for a long moment. Finally, he turned away. "You honestly think I care?" he said gruffly.

At first, she thought she'd misheard him. But the way he shrugged her off made it clear she hadn't. Her ribs felt like walls closing in on each other. She might've stomached those words once, expected them even, but she assumed they were past all that. She thought that day at the teahouse had meant something, had *changed* something. But apparently, she'd been wrong. It felt as if he'd tossed his tarot deck into the air once more—and Aris didn't feel like playing.

With a slow breath, she drew her knees to her chest. She rose to her feet, teetering along the wall before easing herself onto the windowsill. And she did all this with the utmost elegance she could muster. Her swift movements muttered, *I couldn't care less that you couldn't care less.* Or at least they would have if her foot hadn't slipped. She glanced up for only a second, just long enough to glimpse his reaction.

Next thing she knew, her stomach was caught in her chest. There were fingers clutching her wrist, a hand intertwined with her own. Aris blinked up at a pair of pale eyes. *Eyes she'd easily seen a hundred times, one green and the other blue.*

But Lochlen wasn't looking at her like he'd saved her. He was looking at her like she'd turned to leave and he'd asked her to stay. And then, in a slow voice, he said, "Who did you draw first?"

They stayed like that for a moment. Suspended. Him, waiting for a response, and her, knowing he already knew the answer. When his eyes flickered, she thought he was about to confess something of his own, but instead he forced a smile, like the corners of his lips were bound by strings and someone had just given them a firm tug. And then—he dropped her hand.

Aris's heart stopped for a second. She was only about a foot off the ground, and a pair of arms was behind her, quick to brace her shoulders when she stumbled. *Alek.*

"Still getting the hang of your powers, I see," he said with a taunting grin.

Aris gawked at him, but his smile spread, and Aris could feel every inch of it shining down on her. *I would be an idiot to turn him down,* she reminded herself before following him back to where the others had formed a small circle at one edge of the ruins.

Mirai tossed Aris a pillow from the mountain she appeared to be hoarding, and Jada held out the bottle of wine. They passed it around the circle, but when it got to Yuki, he waved it off. He had a book in his hand again, the one they'd stolen from the library. Aris recognized the tiny illustration of a tree near the top of the page. Had he been rereading the same excerpt since yesterday?

"Can I help you?" Yuki said tersely.

Aris's face scrunched. "I just wanted to know what it's about."

"It's about a lost faerie trying to find her way home."

"I thought you said it was poetry?"

Yuki flicked his wrist. "It is and it isn't." He sighed. "Each poem is a continuation of the story."

"So what's this passage about?" Aris asked, pointing at the tree.

"It would seem she's found a ship or some sort of vessel, and yet she's waiting."

"Waiting for what?"

He glanced up, his face askew. "Well, it says . . ." He paused. "The virgin."

Everyone stilled for a moment. "If you're saying we have to make a sacrifice, I nominate Jada," Lochlen proposed from the other side of the castle. Mirai pulled Jada into her arms as if Lochlen had just offered up her only child, and then she was standing.

"There's no way it says that," she crowed, peering over Yuki's shoulder. Squinting, she added, "I forgot this was Welsh. I don't know why I bothered getting up. I recognize a total of one word."

Yuki craned his neck. "Which one?"

"Gwirsiare," Mirai said, sounding out each syllable.

"It's not gwirsiare, it's—holy shit, it's gwirsiare." Yuki's eyes were the size of two moons as he looked between his sister and the book.

But Mirai just shrugged. "Duh."

"Which power is that again?" Jada asked, and Aris suddenly recognized the word as one of the branches from the tree in the crypt.

Yuki looked very small as he said, "You don't understand . . . gwirsiare doesn't translate. It's not Welsh." He cocked his head, eyes darting back and forth. "It's not Welsh," he said again, though this time it was more to himself than anyone else, and when he dropped his gaze, his eyes looked less like moons than two meteorites crashing to earth. "They're not waiting for the virgin at all," he muttered. "They're waiting for the gwirsiare."

"Someone with that specific power?" Alck offered.

"Either that, or the moon."

Aris glanced at the sky, to the moon that, according to the wheel in the crypt, was called the Reaper's Moon. Its light rained down upon the ruined castle, casting long shadows that blurred from the warm glow of tea lights. Some stones appeared more brown than gray, while others looked almost blue, like something out of an eighteenth-century oil painting.

Mirai asked Yuki how he could've confused *gwirsiare* with *virgin* and Yuki was muttering something about mistaking an *a* for a *g* when Aris turned back to him. "Can I see that book for a second?"

"What? No." Yuki jerked backward, his fingers clutching the spine.

"Here," Mirai said, swiping the book from his grasp and tossing it to Aris.

Aris examined the covers, first the front, then the back, but it wasn't until she started picking at the spine that Yuki lurched forward. "What the hell do you think you're doing?" he demanded.

Aris staggered back. "I know, I know. Trust me, I hate this as much as you do, but if you'd just let me finish . . ." With as much precision as her stubby nails would allow, Aris peeled back the topmost layer until the spine turned from red to blue. Underneath the new binding was the original name. *Powell.* But there was something else. She continued scratching away until the lower half of the spine was completely blue, all except for where 'Powell' had been etched in gold, alongside a small emblem. Two crescents on either side of a full moon.

Mirai, clutching Jada's wrist, said, "Is that—?"

Yuki nodded.

Alek's eyes twinkled as he stepped toward her. "How?"

Aris wasn't sure she could answer that question. She flipped through the pages, seeing them in a different light. "Do you remember what I said about the paintings? That researchers have been x-raying them?" He nodded. "I don't know why I thought of it just now, or how it all clicked. It's strange. It's like I just—"

"Knew," Alek and Lochlen said in unison. Aris wasn't sure when Lochlen had joined them, but she could feel both sets of eyes on her now, waiting to see where she'd look first. *To whom* she'd look first. But when Yuki sucked in a breath, it ended up being him she turned to face.

Mirai whirled as well. "What?" she snapped. He pressed his hands to his face. "What?" Mirai was yelling now.

Yuki tore the book from Aris's hands, flipping to the final chapter. "Do think it's possible this book was written by an actual Anathemian?" Mirai quirked her brow. "It's poetry, yes, but it reads almost like a diary. She ends every entry by naming the constellations she falls asleep gazing at. If I cross reference them with the seasons, I might be able to get a rough estimate of her location."

"Which means?"

"Which *means*, we might've just found a literal map to Krysidia."

Mirai dropped Jada's wrist. "No fucking way," she whispered, and then threw a hand over her mouth. A giggle escaped her lips, and it was like a fuse being lit. Aris watched the spark make its way through the circle. Eyes lighting up, one after another. Alek reached for the wine bottle. He clapped Yuki on the shoulder, offering him the first sip, and this time, Yuki accepted it gladly.

Yuki's smile was like a sigh of relief. It was a rainbow at the end of a storm, and suddenly Aris was drunk on pride and hope and maybe a tiny bit of elderflower wine, but mostly the first two. Yuki hadn't found Krysidia, but they were closer now than ever before. Aris could feel it. They all could.

When the bottle made its way back around, Aris turned to offer some to Lochlen, but he was gone. Her heart started to churn. It skidded, then stopped. Aris recognized the feeling. She'd experienced it at least once before—the moment she'd lifted Lochlen's poisonous brew to her lips. The wine bottle slipped from her fingers. It landed on one of the cushions before rolling softly to the ground. It didn't break, but for some reason, she wished it had. Then, a voice in her head said, *Forgive me*.

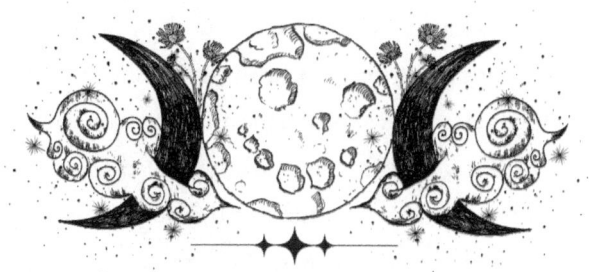

CHAPTER 36

A ris had her back against the wall of the ruins when a man limped through the archway, Evie dragging alongside him. All it took was one glimpse of the gun in his hand, and Aris delved into an altered state of awareness. Her vision was hazy, yet focused. She could see everything in vivid detail, but her brain refused to process any of it. It was a lot like watching a train get derailed—just a giant mess of information that would never get delivered.

She heard Alek exclaim, "You bastard!" and then a stream of muffled laughter from somewhere else.

"I'm sorry, I'm sorry," wheezed the man. "It's just"—a snort—"it's just, well, technically, that would be you, wouldn't it?"

Aris felt Alek's rage boil up beside her. She blinked once, twice, trying to figure out who this man was and how Alek knew him, but she had a hard time looking past the bruised cheek and battered nose to recognize the eyes looking back at her when there was nothing behind them but the repetitive churn of broken gears. A brisk gust pushed the hair from the man's face, and then . . . Aris's voice came out like a whimper. "Mr.—Mr. Matthews?" She was glad for the wall then, glad to have something holding her upright as the rest of the world flipped ninety degrees.

Evie cried out for her sister, and Mr. Matthews jammed the gun against her skull.

Aris could feel everyone's confusion. She felt Yuki's fears, Mirai's revulsion, and Jada's abhorrence at their helplessness. The only person she couldn't seem to feel was Lochlen.

She stared at her teacher, or what had become of him, but all she saw was the rim of a silver goblet. A man filled with resentment. "What are you . . ." she stumbled. "Why are—"

"Isn't it obvious?" Mr. Matthews shrieked, and the noise made her squirm. "I've come to save you." Aris looked between Evie and the gun. "What, this?" He gave the weapon a shake. "No, this is just insurance. You didn't think I was doing this out of the goodness of my heart, did you?" His voice cracked. "No, no, of course not, because whenever I do something out of the goodness of my fucking heart, I end up left for dead on the side of the road. So this time, I intend to collect my dues upfront."

Aris shuddered. She'd never heard a teacher swear before. Then again, she'd never seen one with a gun in his hand, either. She thought of the hairbrush. The thin silver handle crashing to the ground. *Luck. Coincidence. Fate.* The three words rolled around in her head like a set of marbles. Evie's blond hair hung in braids down either side of her neck, her face beet-red, making her green eyes look as if they might pop out of her head. She looked so small. So frail. So innocent. Aris swallowed, remembering the young girl from her vision. She would not—could not—let Evie end up like that.

She would not cry. She would not lunge. Instead, she raised both hands as if calming a wild animal. Slowly, steadily, she asked him, "What do you want?"

Mr. Matthews raised a finger and pointed at Alek. Reactions tugged her in every direction. Panic. Fear. Rage. Not realizing she'd been standing on her toes, Aris fell to the soles of her feet. Leaves crunched beneath them and a second later, the gun was aimed at her instead. But almost as fast as Mr. Matthews flicked his wrist, Alek stepped between them.

"Look at that," Mr. Matthews said, his hand squeezing Evie's arm. "My nephew actually thinks he's being brave. But it's not bravery at all, is it? Not when you're not really putting yourself in danger."

Aris nearly missed it. The word *nephew*. This man, her teacher, was his *uncle*? Everyone suddenly had their eyes glued to Alek instead of the gun.

The teacher threw back his head in a fit of laughter and Aris tensed as the force of the jolt made Evie squint. Then he brushed off his clothes and straightened his collar. "Let me introduce myself properly. My full name," he said, staring at Alek now instead of Aris, "is Harrison Matthew *Davenport*." His eye was still twitching as he said, "You look just like him, you know. My brother."

It took a couple of shallow breaths for her to figure out that the pain in her chest was Alek slowly breaking apart in front of her. The guilt she felt could've brought her to her knees, but Aris forced herself not to crumble. *Has Mr. Matthews known about Alek all along? Has he been searching for him? Have I led Mr. Matthews straight to him?* None of it seemed real.

A scrape of metal, and Mirai bared her teeth, moving to jump, katana outstretched. *No*, Aris wanted to scream as the teacher tightened his grip on Evie and returned his gun to her temple.

But Mr. Matthews simply cackled. "Oh look, the warrior's itching for a fight. Better keep that temper of yours under control. I bet you're fast, but are you faster than one of these bullets?" He glanced over his gun and then raised a brow. "Care to wager on it?" Yuki hauled his sister back by her sleeve, his lips twisting.

"Aris, I'm sorry," Evie broke off. "Garret said—Garret said you were in trouble. He said he needed my help."

"Garret?" Aris's voice shriveled.

Mr. Matthews snapped his fingers. When nothing happened, he craned his head. "Garret!" The boy walked forward slowly, clutching something against his chest. The sketchbook landed just in front of Aris's feet, its pages splayed open to the drawing of Mirai, who blushed furiously upon seeing it. "I noticed you didn't include Evie in your little tribute." Mr. Matthews tapped a finger to his mouth. "Is that a bit of sibling rivalry I'm sensing?"

"What? No! Please. Please, just let her go." The tear that escaped Aris's eye was too well timed, and for a moment, she worried it looked fake. But Mr. Matthews hadn't seemed to notice. It occurred to her then that he wasn't seeing her at all. His mind was somewhere else. And that fact scared her more than anything.

"He would've killed you, you know. *All* of you."

"Who would've?" Jada squeaked.

Mr. Matthews clicked his tongue. "Not so fast. This is a negotiation, remember? I'm not giving you any more information until I get what I came for." He turned to Alek again. "I *want* my brother's ring."

"And what if we don't *want* your information?" Yuki countered.

"Then I'll kill Evie and take her crystal instead." The teacher shrugged. "Up to you."

Aris didn't point out that Evie didn't have a crystal. She couldn't risk provoking him. And while all her instincts were telling her Mr. Matthews wouldn't actually go through with it, she wasn't completely sure she believed it. Because the man standing in front of her was no longer her history teacher. He was what was left of him. Which was why when Yuki said, "He's bluffing," the color drained from her face.

Mr. Matthews gaped. "Am I?"

Aris's scream came out in large, breathless sobs as Mr. Matthews pulled the trigger. Yuki dropped to the ground, his face an echo of everyone else's horror.

A split second later, Mr. Matthews burst into laughter. "The safety's still on, see?" He fingered the trigger as if it were a toy, and then smacked a hand to his head. "You should've seen your faces."

Mirai shot forward again, but a small click halted her in her tracks. The sound of the safety being disabled.

"I'll give it to you," Alek blurted. "Just let her go." He glanced back at Aris, giving her a look that said everything was going to be fine, and then took off his ring, holding it out for Mr. Matthews to claim.

Mr. Matthews nodded to Garret, who reached for a bundle of sage before plucking the ring from Alek's hand. Smoke wafted over the metal and Aris pictured Alek's energy slowly dissolving.

She stared at Alek's empty hand.

Just like that, all his dreams had been shattered. And all Aris could think about was how selfish she was. She'd been so worried about telling her sister, and if she had, maybe they wouldn't be in this situation. Maybe Alek wouldn't be giving up his powers to save her.

Aris dug her nails into the fabric of her dress as Garret wormed the ring onto Mr. Matthews's finger. *This is ridiculous.* Six Anathemians up against one man. There had to be something one of them could do. She looked to Jada, but one slight shake of their head told her everything. They couldn't heal a bullet to the head. At least not fast enough.

Guns are so unfair.

"You have what you wanted. Now let her go," Alek growled, the frown on his face boiling into something more vicious.

"How many times do I have to say this? I'm here to save you. See?" Mr. Matthews held his hand up in the air, flaunting the ring like a newly engaged bride. "I'm a protector now."

"And how exactly do you intend to save us?"

The teacher sighed. "The man who's after you—Brax—well, he's not going to stop until he tracks you down. He doesn't care that you're children, or that my brother was his best friend. He's greedy and callous, and"—Mr. Matthews cleared his throat—"*and* our only option now is . . . well, is Krysidia." He said *Krysidia* as if presenting the answer to an unsolved equation.

Alek uncurled his fist. "You know where it is?"

Mr. Matthews's eyes rolled back. "Not exactly, but I'm close, and I figured—" Perhaps they'd been too quiet. Perhaps someone's gaze had dropped, or their breath had caught, but Mr. Matthews seemed to have picked up on something. "Unless . . . you've already found it?" There was a hint of accusation in his tone.

Aris jerked her chin. "Found what?"

"The door to Krysidia. You've already found it." He burst into laughter again. "Of course you have. Knowing my brother, I bet he stumbled upon it by accident." Spit flew off his lips as he spoke. "Of course, of course, of course," Mr. Matthews continued, "because *he* never cared about finding it. So *of course* that's exactly what happened." He delved into a maniacal rant about his brother failing to appreciate his gift, the gun jerking in beat with his words. Evie flinched each time the barrel moved, and Aris felt the anxiety bubble up from her sister's stomach. She couldn't take it anymore.

"You seriously think we know where it is?" she spat.

Mr. Matthews blinked. "Well, do you?"

"Of course not," she screamed. "Why the hell would we still be here if we did?"

Mr. Matthews smiled like he knew something she didn't, and then he turned to her sister. "Evie, dear, are they lying to me?" Evie's lips wobbled, but she kept them shut. Mr. Matthews took a long, strangled breath, the gun trembling in his hand. He wiped his face with his arm and repeated the question, this time shouting the words.

Evie looked up at Aris, her expression mournful. "Yes," she admitted.

Mr. Matthews twitched again. "See, here's the thing. Evie, here, is a truthseeker. And not only do truthseekers know whether someone else is being honest, but they're also unequivocally honest themselves." He smirked. "That's what makes them the ultimate lie detectors."

CHAPTER 37

Waiting for a vision was like being suffocated—strangled by your own breath until it came to pass. But worse than that was waiting for a vision you hoped would never come. *Is this what it feels like to drown?* Lochlen thought. *Holding your breath until your head hurts so badly that it decides to shut off?*

From his spot atop the tower, he'd seen everything, and it took all he had to stay there, even as Alek's uncle jammed a gun to Evie's head, even as Alek gave up the ring, even as Aris disappeared into the forest with the lunatic and his lapdog. A hero might've swooped down just in the nick of time, might've made a big show of saving the day. But if he was honest, the word never really suited him.

From the moment Lochlen's feet hit the ground, Mirai had her sword at his throat. "Where were you?" she choked, fighting back tears. Behind her, Alek's eyes were two burning balls of fire.

"Did you know?" he demanded, his chin dipping to Evie, the girl now hovering at his side. Lochlen glanced at the blade still raised. "Did you know?" Alek barked again.

Lochlen took a steeling breath. "No," he said, wishing it weren't the truth. He wished he'd predicted Evie's part in all this, wished he'd been able to prevent it. He wished he'd at least told Aris when he'd first suspected her sister's powers.

Mirai lowered her sword. "Wait, did you know someone was after Alek's ring?" Lochlen and Alek shared a glance as she returned her katana to its sheath. "You did, didn't you?"

Lochlen's silence might as well have been a confession, and before he knew it, he was bombarded with questions.

"Did you know Alek had an uncle?" Jada asked.

"Did you know he would have a gun?" Mirai added.

"Did you know he would take Aris?"

"Did you know she knew where to find the portal?"

Then Yuki dragged himself to his feet. "Did you know the reaper was working with the man who killed my aunt?" he asked, his voice like sandpaper.

Even before he'd met them, Lochlen knew he'd have secrets his friends could never know. He knew they'd have questions he couldn't answer. Lochlen believed in fate almost as much as he believed in his ability to change it, but he also knew that the more people involved, the harder the future became to control. Telling his friends the truth, warning them, preparing them—it certainly would've changed the future. The problem was, there was no telling if it'd be for the better. This version may not have been perfect, but at least they'd all survived.

And for that, Lochlen knew his own happiness had been but a small price to pay.

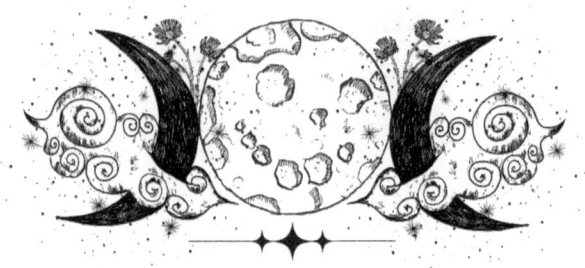

CHAPTER 38

Mr. Matthews's car was not a villain car. It was a Corolla. And until about an hour ago, her history teacher had looked exactly like the type of person who would drive a Corolla, but not anymore. Not since he'd pointed a gun at her little sister and robbed Alek of his magic.

"Northwest," Aris said. These were the first instructions that came to mind—the only instructions, actually. She fiddled with the seatbelt currently scraping her collarbone until it threatened to strangle her.

Truthseeker. The word resonated as they drove. Mr. Matthews seemed pretty convinced of Evie's powers, but Aris was still on the fence. She knew it was possible for both siblings to inherit a crystal. Mirai and Yuki were proof of that. She also knew Evie was impeccable at detecting lies.

Only, Aris hadn't lied when she said she didn't know where the portal was.

A piece of hair fell over her eye, and Aris swatted at it. She wished Alek were here, though part of her was glad he'd been forced to stay behind. Mr. Matthews had gawked at Alek for his faux bravery at the ruins, but Aris was pretty sure he would've stepped between her and that gun even without his magic.

Through the sideview mirror, she could see her teacher fiddling with his ring. It was unbelievable, really. In some twisted delusion, Mr. Matthews still considered himself to be the hero. She felt it like a crown atop his head. He sat there basking in his self-righteousness, even though all he'd done was wave a gun around, kidnap Evie, steal Alek's ring, and then take her hostage. And now *she* was the one leading *him* to Krysidia. Or at least, she was supposed to be.

Aris rubbed her eyes. Her only conclusion was that somewhere in that poetry book was a map, just as Yuki suggested.

She stifled a groan as the car pulled up to a red light, and part of her considered making a run for it. Mr. Matthews had lowered the gun when they got into the city, which meant technically there was nothing keeping her here. *Nothing except Alek's ring.* And then there was Garret. They may have been on opposite sides, but Aris had seen his hands tremble as he'd reached for that stick of sage, and she couldn't bring herself to leave the kid at Mr. Matthews's mercy, even if he had used his power to literally stalk her for the last several days.

She pressed her forehead to the window, staring at a bright red sign directing her to the nearest bank, and then at the slightly larger blue billboard with a picture of an accountant captioned with the jaunty phrase, "We're here to help." Aris rolled her eyes. The street itself looked an awful lot like the one where The Twisted Juniper resided, though she knew it wasn't. This street was made of suffocatingly perfect cubes, all lined up in a row, while that street had felt like crooked roofs and weeds pushing up between sidewalk cracks, as if it were the banks that didn't belong . . .

Holy shit.

Aris reached for the map tucked into the seat pocket in front of her. The first dot she made marked the ruins, the second, The Twisted Juniper. It was something Lochlen had said. His weird exchange with the reaper. *The best way to avoid a ghost is to get off the grid.* Ghosts must be limited to the ley lines, or at least, stronger on them. She was surprised Lochlen hadn't made the connection sooner.

Lochlen. A sharp pain settled in the back of her throat. If she thought too hard about his decision to stay hidden up in his tower, her head would likely explode.

Aris quietly cleared her throat and used the edge of an old coffee sleeve to connect the ruins and the shop. She extended the line upward, but when she got to the mountains, she paused. Truthseeker. The word nipped at her again. When Alek first took her through the mountains, she'd been so discouraged. She'd barely believed in her powers, let alone trusted them. Then she'd been so hesitant about Krysidia; she hadn't *wanted* to find it. Of course, now that she had no choice, the signs were so painfully obvious. The tree she'd seen in the mountains hadn't been trying to lead her to the book. It was the opposite.

There were four points outside the city where her estimation of the ley line intersected with the road, but it wasn't until they reached the third that Aris saw it.

The tree was every bit as decrepit as she remembered, its branches curling over the way a wave barrels back into the ocean. But where originally, it looked as though it was cowering from whizzing cars, now it looked like it was protecting something.

Hiding something.

CHAPTER 39

"You didn't tell me it was underground," Mr. Matthews griped. "We can't just go caving, you know. We need ropes, protective gloves. For god's sake, we don't even have headlamps." He'd been counting on his fingers when his voice cracked, and Aris didn't know if it was out of fear or annoyance.

Her eyes grew wide. For someone so desperate for magic, he seemed awfully skeptical of it.

Aris dragged her hand along the side of the mountain and said, "For some reason, I don't think we'll be needing any." She plucked a loose branch no taller than her waist and studied the stone wall behind it. First, she reached out a hand. Then, she grinned slowly. *Just as I suspected.*

Aris glanced back to ensure both Garret and Mr. Matthews were watching and then she charged headfirst through the tree—*through* the side of the mountain. Or at least, that's what it must've looked like. The truth was, everything Yuki mentioned about meridians was accurate. The light in this place was just as contorted as the tree. Even at night, it warped to make the opening of the cave appear solid.

For a moment, she stood alone inside the cavern, tapping her stick against the ground, her smile growing with every knock. She was a freaking genius.

When Garret was the first to follow her inside, Aris frowned, her tongue pressed to her cheek. Though there wasn't enough time for it to be awkward. He rushed forward, forcing her back until her elbow connected with the stone wall behind her. "Aris, listen to me," he whispered furiously. "Mr. Matthews told me Aleksander was part of a gang that hunts down other Anathemians. He said he was trying to recruit you. That's why I stole your sketchbook. That's why I went to Evie, why she came with me. I honestly thought I was helping you."

Her breath caught in her throat as her mind scrambled to process his words. "Okay, but then why—"

"He may have lied about Aleksander, but the gang is real," Garret panted. "And they know about the ruins."

She pressed her lips together and then clamped a hand over his sleeve. "Do you have your phone?"

"No. He—"

Mr. Matthews slipped through the entrance, and Garret went silent. He backed away, and Aris stooped to retrieve the stick she'd dropped when Garret ran at her. The teacher eyed them, and then, for the first time since leaving the ruins, he raised his gun.

All Aris could think was, *Even when you think you're going to die, you don't actually* think *you're going to die.* She tugged at her sleeve, but something caught at the hem. She looked down to see a chain of suns and stars and moons. A sudden weightlessness washed over her. She hadn't felt Lochlen slip it over her hand, but it had to have been some time tonight. Her own words came back to her in a whirl. *You can give it back, once I know it's not going to kill me.*

Maybe she was reading too much into this. Or maybe ... Had Lochlen been trying to reassure her? To tell her she would make it out of here? That everything was going to be okay? She took a breath. Had he known she would be taken? That she'd know where to find the portal?

Aris tucked the bracelet beneath her sleeve and straightened the rest of her dress. She stared down the barrel of the gun and gripped her stick, wishing it were a sword, trying to remember the feeling she'd gotten when she touched that model ship. But the cave was a mess of anxiety and suspicion, both of which made her stomach churn.

The tunnel ahead was dark, but not as dark as it should have been. A blue glow emitted from the walls, guiding them through the cavern, and while Aris's first few steps were steep, the rest was a gradual descent, like a staircase winding downward.

The walls began rustling as they walked, like a thousand lost souls whispering all at once, and Aris found herself humming along to the rhythm that muffled the sound of Mr. Matthews's leg dragging behind him.

She needed to get out of here, to warn the others. But Mr. Matthews still had Alek's ring . . . Although, what good would it do if Alek was already dead? Once again, she felt backed into a corner. Once again, both options were dark and uncharted. Once again, she felt herself fumbling for a loose stone or a hidden lever, wasting her time waiting for a magical solution instead of facing her decisions head on.

Just as she was starting to doubt fate altogether, the tunnel opened to a sandy shore, disappearing beneath a pool so blue it couldn't have been anything less than magic. Any remaining doubts were quashed by the familiar symbol carved into the stone wall across the water: two crescents, one on either side of the full moon, the center of which glowed faintly, like the beam of a distant flashlight.

The nearby walls were covered in various carvings, what looked like a short phrase in at least a dozen different languages. She scanned them until she located the English variant. *Beware the broken moon.* Aris returned her attention to the faint glow filling the circle in the center of the wall. Before she'd taken his book away, Yuki said the story told of someone waiting for the gwirsiare in order to make the journey home. Aris bit her lip. She'd bet anything they were referring to the Gwirsiare Moon, that they needed it to use the portal. Her mind blipped to Mirai outside the dojo: *It's when our powers are the strongest.* Yuki said the portal was unstable, that traversing it would be like trying to hold a bridge together and cross it at the same time. If they were relying on their crystals to keep the portal stable, it made sense that the night of the full moon would be the safest time to travel.

Well, shit. If Yuki were here, he probably could've figured out exactly how much time they had. For all she knew, they could be down to a couple hours. *Shit. Shit. Shit.* Her heart pounded, emphasizing each passing second. It was the same feeling she'd had when Alek first demonstrated his powers, the feeling of watching the orange convertible make its way around the bend, of knowing she couldn't make it to him in time.

Aris swallowed, hoping her teacher hadn't noticed the inscriptions. Knowing the portal had a time limit would only magnify his impulsiveness.

The closer they got to the water, the clearer it became. The lake was like one giant rippling mirror, and Aris found herself unable to look away, even as she stared at her own reflection. Even as her own reflection didn't quite stare back. It was for this reason that when Mr. Matthews's reflection lowered his gun, his face bewildered, Aris turned slightly, double checking his actions. "How do I—How uh . . ." He was clearly struggling to frame his own question.

Crouching, Aris skimmed her palm across the water. In her dream—or rather, her nightmare—the door to Krysidia had been a literal door, a thought that seemed ridiculous to her now. Because those types of doors were constructed by humans. This gateway was born of the earth. It existed long before them, and would remain long after. She scooped a hand through the lake, but it was like trying to capture a ray of light. She felt the water against her fingers, and yet the moment she raised them, it was as if nothing had happened. They came out empty, dry, slightly heavier, although that last part could've been an illusion. Despite the impossibility of it all, Aris let her gaze drift from shore to wall, and then, with complete confidence, she said, "You swim."

She felt the gun at her head again. The gesture didn't scare her as much as it had the first time. Mr. Matthews barked, "Don't be stupid, okay? How do I know this isn't a trick?"

Aris watched her words this time. Watched her tone. "Have you ever seen water glow like this?" she asked, gesturing to the lake. "This cave should be pitch black, but it's not. My hands should be wet, but they're dry. Because this water isn't water at all—it's energy." She dipped another finger into the viscous liquid, almost laughing. "I mean, the walls are practically singing."

A glimpse of concern flickered in Mr. Matthews's eyes before he turned. He moved closer to the edge of the cave, one ear facing the wall as he pretended to examine the stone. Aris found herself wondering just how long that ring needed to be on his finger before it started working.

She caught Garret's eye. But where Mr. Matthews's gaze had wavered, Garret was unblinking. She felt his desperation to help her, to make up for getting her into this. And he knew as well as she did that they could still win.

Aris nodded, slowly, adjusting her grip on her stick until her right hand was at a forty-five-degree angle, and a proper distance from her left. Then, with all her strength, she struck the back of Mr. Matthews's bad leg, sending him howling to the ground. Garret barreled forward, knocking the gun from Mr. Matthews's hand as he scrambled to pin him down.

The ring. She needed to get the ring.

Aris tossed her stick to the side and leaped for Mr. Matthews's hand. He balled his fingers into a fist, and she struggled to unfurl them as Garret wrestled him against the sand. The grit clung to her clammy hands as she peeled back Mr. Matthews's thumb. But then, with the flash of an elbow, Garret rolled to one side, gasping. Aris didn't wait for Mr. Matthews to shake her off. Instead, she lunged past him, unaware of what she was grasping for until she was holding it.

The gun felt wrong in her hands. It reeked of fear and anger and corruption, like metal should never be formed this way. The earth didn't want it. It wished it had the power to undo it.

"That was a mistake," Mr. Matthews spat, dragging himself up against the wall. "In case you've forgotten," he heaved, "I'm immune to your bullets." His words echoed through the cave, and so did his doubt.

"Obviously, that power of yours hasn't quite kicked in yet." She tightened her grip on the gun. He deserved this. He had placed this gun to Evie's head. He had forced Alek to give up his ring, and now she would show him how it felt to be on the receiving end of the barrel. She turned her head to Garret but kept her eyes on Mr. Matthews. "If you're going to cross, go now." It could've been 2 a.m. or 5 a.m., and if her hunch was right, they either had to cross now, or wait until the next full moon. She remembered what Mirai had said about her aunt being able to trace people, but how her powers had been useless against an attack. "That gang, they know about you too, right?" Garret stilled, and Aris felt his attention shift to Mr. Matthews. "Go," she mouthed, finally looking at him.

She felt his reluctance as he dipped his feet into the water, but it was smothered by a thick cloud sparking with jealousy. Mr. Matthews balled his hands into fists again, rage ripping through him as he watched someone else pursue his dream.

"I'll tell her what happened," Aris soothed, pushing through Mr. Matthews's anger to feel the edges of Garret's grief. It seeped out of him. A slow gray essence, just like the pocket watch she'd found at the antique shop. "I'll tell her you made it back," she added, her voice breaking. Aris forced herself to smile. "She'll be so proud of you."

Those six words were the gentle push he needed, and when Garret disappeared beneath the surface, the only sound she heard was Mr. Matthews collapsing to the ground in big wet sobs. "Please. Please, I'm nothing without this ring."

It was unsettling how pathetic he looked now. How quickly he'd gone from threatening her to groveling at her feet. *And how easily she'd done the opposite.* Aris shook off the thought, and then, with a breath, she said, "That's not true." She tilted her head. "Before that ring, you were my favorite teacher."

He lurched forward, his fingers digging into the sand. "I wasn't going to shoot her, I promise." Mr. Matthews jerked a hand and sand flew everywhere. He punched the ground repeatedly. "I just wanted to feel safe again. I swear. I didn't want to hurt anyone."

"Except Alek," Aris bit back.

The teacher sniffled as he wiped his face of tears. "Brax doesn't know his face." His voice was laced with desperation. "If he leaves now, Brax will never find him."

"And where the hell is he supposed to go?"

Mr. Matthews raised one hand like a white flag, and slowly reached into his pocket. Aris watched him carefully. He pulled out a crumpled piece of paper and held it out. "My brother is a tricky man to find, but I had Garret track him down." He traded hands, so the one holding the note was the one without the ring. "Let me keep the ring, and my brother's whereabouts are yours."

His family in exchange for his magic. How the hell was she supposed to make a decision like *that*?

"Finding his dad doesn't exonerate you for stealing his ring," Aris finally said.

"Well, if you don't want it . . ." Mr. Matthews let his mouth hang open, drawing the paper up to his lips. He was cockier now, and Aris didn't like it.

"I could still shoot you, you know."

He paused, the note still in his hand. "Go ahead. My life's purpose was to find Krysidia, and now that I've found it . . . well, I think I'd rather die than give it up."

He really has lost it.

Aris glanced over the man she thought she'd known. A man she'd thought she could trust. Once again, she found herself questioning just how much they inherited from their ancestors, and if she could've ended up just like him.

Maybe she already had.

Aris remembered the gun in her hand, and her skin began to crawl. Maybe she was only good because she hadn't had a reason to be anything else. Mr. Matthews had certainly given her a reason, and in that moment, she realized how much easier it was to hurt someone who'd hurt you first.

She thought of Alek. Alek, sitting at a dive bar on the south side of town, waiting for someone to pick a fight. She understood him now more than ever. The way he'd justified his actions. But she also knew that once his anger was gone, those justifications went with it. It was guilt he woke up with, not pride.

With a breath, she disarmed the gun, making sure Mr. Matthews saw her flip the safety on before trudging over and snatching the note from his hand. "*I* found it," she corrected as she memorized the address. "Not you. *Me*." She refolded the page and tucked it into the side of her boot. "And you're still alive because I'm letting you live. You better hope that whatever is on the other side of the portal is just as merciful."

When she turned to head back through the tunnel, she expected to hear a splash, but she didn't, and for a split second, she was hopeful. But when she looked back, her teacher was gone. The cavern was still. And she was alone.

The trek to the surface felt long and heavy. The weight of the gun in her hand dragged her down. It disrupted her instincts like a magnetic field making a compass spin. *I need to warn them*, she thought, each word another step forward. Another foot closer to the mouth of the cave. When she finally reached it, she expected to see the sun starting to rise. But the outside of the cave was even darker than the inside, and she could barely see her own two feet as she felt her way through the branches.

Aris leaned back against Mr. Matthews's car, silently cursing herself for sending Garret through the portal with their teacher's keys. She turned, one hand pressed to her face in exasperation, but as she glanced over the vehicle, the sweat clamming up her hands turned cold. Where she'd expected to see only one reflection in the side mirror, there were two.

For the second time that night, Aris drew the gun.

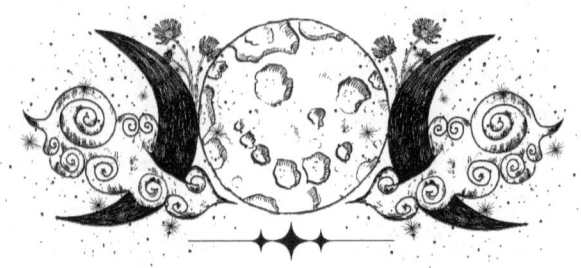

CHAPTER 40

"What are you going to do? Shoot me?" It was Lochlen. He was leaning against the mountain, utterly unfazed by the gun pointed at his head. In that moment, she couldn't remember if she trusted him or hated him, if she was mad or grateful. In that moment, all she could think was, *It was Lochlen.*

Her breath hitched as she dropped the gun. She stood there a moment, lip wobbling. Then she was running. She pressed her cheek against his chest, buried her fingers in his sweater. At first, Lochlen's shoulders tensed, and she half expected him to push her away, but then his arms softened and molded to her shape. He held her gently at first, and then fiercely, like he never wanted to let her go. He was holding her like he *knew* her, and Aris c that feeling.

She wanted to know.

She *needed* to know.

Aris blinked up at him, at his eyes. *His* eyes. One green. One blue. Both staring down at her. She held her breath, her mind flooding with a string of images. A boy with those eyes sitting atop a reddened roof. A boy with those eyes running through a garden of blue hydrangeas. A boy with those eyes drifting to sleep on the edge of a silk rug, smiling at the base of an ash tree, catching her at the foot of a cliff. Aris opened her own eyes then. Ones she hadn't remembered closing. Without thinking, she smiled up at him. "Found you," she whispered.

Lochlen's gaze went glossy. He stopped breathing. He said nothing. Instead, he reached into his pocket, pulling out a carefully folded piece of paper. The corner caught the moonlight before he could unfold it, and Aris's heart pounded as she remembered all that had happened. "The gang. They know about the ruins," she blurted. "Where are the others? Are they still there?"

Lochlen shook his head, the paper still folded between his fingers. "Alek took everyone to Yuki and Mirai's."

Aris knocked her head back in relief, only for reality to hit her again, this time like an anvil. "How long has the moon been full for?"

Lochlen raised his wrist halfway, only to drop it again. "Six, maybe seven hours since its peak, why?"

"Shit." Aris rummaged her pockets for her phone, only to remember it was locked in Mr. Matthews' car. "I think the portal only works during the full moon." She clawed at her sleeves, failing to pull the stiff fabric over her hands. "Which means if you don't leave soon you'll all be stuck here another month, and—" she sucked in a breath. "And—" Her hand jittered as she brought it up to cover her mouth. Lochlen curled his fingers around her wrist, steadying it. "Alek's ring . . ." Aris shook her head. "I-I couldn't get it back." Her words came out in short spurts.

Lochlen tucked a piece of hair behind her ear. "It was never your job to get it back," he soothed.

She staggered backward, letting his hands fall away. "What?"

He still seemed a bit dazed as he clarified, "The ring your teacher took wasn't real."

She looked down at the bracelet again, unsure if *relieved* was the right word for what she was feeling. "You knew?"

Lochlen nodded, though he looked more scared than smug.

Another step, and this time, Aris's voice came out like ice. "You knew someone was after Alek's ring, and your big plan was to sulk up in that tower, watching the whole thing play out like some sick omniscient god?" She choked out a humorless laugh. "You *knew*, and you let me go off with that lunatic, thinking he'd just destroyed Alek's life?" The gun she dropped had been reduced to a dark scuff against the pavement, but she stared at it as if it were a statue towering a hundred feet in the air.

Her stomach felt like a towel being wrung to dry.

"You wouldn't have shot him," Lochlen said.

"You don't know that," Aris whimpered, her voice barely audible.

She'd been so close to pulling that trigger, so close to ending his life and then prying the ring from his cold, lifeless finger. *So. Close.*

Lochlen rushed forward, taking her face in his hands. "I've never been surer of anything." He leaned down, gently tilting her chin. "That's not who you are," he said, and Aris stopped breathing entirely. He used his thumb to wipe a tear from her cheek and then laughed ever so softly. "You and these damn tears."

She felt like she was looking at two different people—one safe and familiar, the other cold and manipulative. The problem was, she didn't know which was real. She closed her eyes, trying not to think about the feeling of his fingers on her face, or the words she so desperately wanted to believe. Instead, she broke away from him again. "Did you know about Evie?"

"Aris, I—"

"Did you know he was going to use her as leverage?" Aris bit out.

Lochlen stared down for a while, his eyes glued to the last few surviving flowers woven through her laces. And then he took the folded piece of paper and slipped it back into his pocket. She hadn't been prepared for his answer. Hadn't expected him to say yes. And yet, that was the word he eventually forced out. The word that changed everything.

Aris couldn't look at him. She didn't *want* to look at him. Not like she had been. Not now, not ever.

Chapter 41

The moon wasn't waiting. It didn't care that they had families they weren't ready to leave, or beds they might've wanted to sleep in one last time. It didn't care how tired they were, or how badly they needed to shower. It didn't care that tonight might've been the best and worst night of Aris's life, and it certainly did not care what would happen to them if they ended up stuck in Elsley for another month.

Aris needed to pack. No, she needed to say goodbye to her parents. No, she needed to write everything out. As she put pen to paper, she remembered the note Alek received from his father, how long it seemed and yet how little it actually explained. She hated knowing she was doing the exact same thing to her dads. They deserved better than the words she scratched across the back of one of her drawings.

Between Lochlen dropping her off and Alek arriving to pick her up, she managed to change her clothes and toss a couple of things into a bag for her and Evie. She climbed into Alek's car, reaching for his wrist. "Are you sure this one's real?" she asked, running her stiff fingers over the ring that had reappeared since she'd last seen him.

Alek flexed his hand. "Pretty sure." The look Aris gave him said, *Pretty sure?* With a chuckle, he added, "I'd offer to lie down in the road again, but we're kind of crunched for time."

Aris dropped his hand, smiling a little as she shook her head. "Just drive."

In the back seat, Evie craned her neck as far back as it could go, her fist squeezing around what Aris assumed was a crystal at the end of a long silver chain. Her eyes remained glued to the spot where their home was, long after it was out of view, the silence giving Aris the feeling of walking on eggshells. She'd expected her sister to protest their departure, or at least question it. Instead, she acted as if the gun was still pressed to her skull, and Aris wondered if that was the type of feeling that ever truly went away.

Wind sent thick clouds of leaves scraping over the hood of the car as they made their way through the mountains, and by the time Alek pulled up behind the twins' silver hatchback, it had started spitting. Lochlen leaned against the side of the trunk with his hood up as Mirai paced back and forth along the road. Through her window, Aris could see Jada trying to calm Mirai, while Yuki stood off to one side, eyes fixed on the gangly tree.

Aris swung a small backpack over her shoulder as she closed the car door. A heartbeat. Then Mirai's arms were draped around her shoulders, Aris's body pinned between her friend and the matte black exterior.

"That selfish son of a bitch!" Mirai pulled away, scanning her over for injuries. She had changed too, her burgundy gown replaced with leggings and an oversized army jacket. "If he'd laid a finger on you, I swear to god I would've—" She made a crushing motion with her fingers, and Aris couldn't help the smile slowly consuming her face.

"Can we get on with it already?" Yuki droned from the other end of the car. "The full moon won't last forever, you know." When Aris looked over, he avoided her gaze. How many times had he replayed that moment in his head? How long would the guilt weigh on him? Yuki had been right about Mr. Matthews's bluff. She knew that now. She'd seen him grovel in the sand. Her teacher had certainly been desperate enough to shoot someone, but in the end, he wouldn't have had the stomach. No doubt, Yuki still blamed himself—as if the gun had actually been fired, as if Evie had actually died.

Beside Yuki, Lochlen was scanning the mountainside, but just looking at him sent a bolt of pain through her chest. Had he known the emotional scars he would be leaving? Had he even cared? Lochlen met her gaze then, as if he'd been listening. But for someone who knew everything, he looked disturbingly caught off guard.

A flash of lightning, and the rain turned from sprinkle to downpour. Lochlen shouted as a rock the size of a microwave came crashing to the road. Then another. Alek yelled for everyone to follow Aris. Not yet used to being the leader, she grabbed Evie's hand and bounded for the mouth of the cave. Fighting the urge to slow down as they neared the tree, Aris closed her eyes. *It's not really there*, she reminded herself as she dove through what she prayed was still just an illusion.

"What the bloody hell was that?" Mirai panted as she, Aris, and Evie stumbled into the cave. Jada and Yuki came next, followed by Lochlen, and finally, Alek.

Aris might've had a guess, and judging by his expression, so did Lochlen, though neither of them said it out loud. Neither of them wanted to add the word *ghost* to the already massive pile of chaos this night had been. Luckily, the rest of them were distracted by the walls and their faint blue glow. They were distracted by the adrenaline and the magic and the impossibility of it all.

Aris strolled forward like a tour guide leading them to the next section of a museum, and they followed her like a group of school children on a field trip, all wide eyed and attempting to maintain a single-file line. As they walked, there was no talk of goodbyes or what would be waiting for them on the other side, nothing but a silent understanding they all shared that there was no turning back now.

When the cave opened to reveal the shimmering lake, Aris heard multiple breaths catch. Even though she'd just been here, it felt different this time, and not just because there was no longer a madman babbling with a gun. The symbol carved above the waterline had changed. Where the faint glow used to bleed generously over the moon in the middle, the light was now off kilter. In a way, it reminded her of an hourglass—and it was down to its last few grains of sand. Yuki gave Aris a slight nod, confirming her suspicions about the moon. It was a good thing they arrived when they did. She stepped forward to join Mirai on the shore.

"So this is it," Mirai announced. "The infamous door to Krysidia." She crossed her arms. "Not much of a door, is it?"

Aris smirked. "Nope." She watched their reflections in the water, Jada's coming into view on her right.

"How deep do you think it goes?" they asked wearily. Aris shrugged. "Well, how long will it take to get across?"

"Hard to say," Aris answered, wondering how she had become the prophet they went to for answers.

"But how—"

"Have a little faith, won't you?" Lochlen crept up beside them, one hand raised, and Aris thought he might give Jada a brotherly pat on the shoulder.

She thought wrong.

Jada went flying face first into the water. Aris jolted, still not used to the unnatural silence of the splash.

"What was that for?" Jada sputtered, dragging themself to shore.

"You know exactly what that was for," Lochlen said, his eyes freshly sharpened.

Mirai leaned into Aris, whispering something about Jada kissing Lochlen's brother right in front of him, before receiving an equally pointed look from Lochlen. The girls both averted their gaze.

Hesitantly, Jada rose to their feet. They moved to wring out their clothes and gasped, patting a hand down their still-dry tunic.

Mirai dipped her fingers into the lake. "What the . . ." She shook her hand as she raised it. Several feet away, Yuki was less vocal, but probably more fascinated than anyone. He took after his sister, first dipping in a hand, then a foot, then a hand again.

Alek was on the other side of the cave. He and Evie were both propped against the wall, and Aris got the sense her sister was more nervous than she'd originally let on. Aris moved to join them, pausing when she overheard Evie say, "So you really can't be injured?"

"So you really can't lie?" Alek countered.

Aris watched them both raise their eyebrows, both look each other over, and then . . . "Magic is pretty cool," Evie concluded.

Alek smirked. "Yeah, it is." He caught Aris's gaze and pushed off the wall. "So, what's the plan?"

Together, all seven of them huddled along the shore, staring not at the water, but at Lochlen. The gloomy boy rolled his eyes. "For fuck's sake. Do you really think I'd let us get this far if I didn't think it was safe?"

That was it. That was all they needed.

Alek grinned. "On the count of three, then."

Mirai shouted, "Onetwothree!" and everyone took off like a group of kids jumping off the dock at somebody's cabin.

Aris held her breath a moment before going under, two moments before realizing she didn't have to. Hesitantly, she inhaled. Something filled her lungs, something that gave the illusion of oxygen.

Mirai appeared beside her, once again looking more mermaid than warrior. She ran a hand through Aris's hair as if strumming a harp and then mouthed something Aris couldn't quite make out. But before she could respond, the others waved them forward.

Aris kicked as hard as she could, but moving through the water—energy—whatever it was—felt like wading through quicksand. Each kick was met by resistance, and every arm thrust utterly slowed.

When Evie tugged on her sleeve, Aris couldn't tell how much time had passed, only that the way back seemed to have blurred, and the way ahead was slightly clearer. She'd lost sight of everyone except Alek, the panic of which drove her forward.

Together, the three of them broke through the surface. Her chest felt a thousand times lighter as she dragged herself onto sand and collapsed at Alek's side. He nudged her arm with his, either to thank her for finding the portal or to make sure she was still alive. Aris nudged him back, either to say, *You're welcome*, or, *Just barely*, and then she rolled onto her shoulder. Alek rolled too. It was a small, intimate gesture that managed to set her nerves ablaze. One second, they were side by side, and the next, they were face to face. One second, he was smiling, and the next . . . he was kissing her.

He was kissing her, and then he wasn't. She couldn't be sure who pulled away, only that one of them had, and the moment she opened her eyes, her gaze drifted past Alek's golden complexion to see Lochlen hauling himself onto the sand. Lochlen dropped his head, letting his hair fall over his eyes, the gesture knocking Aris from the cloud she'd been floating on.

She shot up, looking first for Evie, and then for the others. That's when it hit her. Garret. He'd gone through the portal the same as them, and as far as she knew, his ring had been real. But it was just the seven of them—in a cave that looked eerily similar to the one they'd just ventured from. No trace of the boy who used to race her to the top of the playground. Wherever he was, she hoped he was safe.

Mirai—as the only one of them with energy to spare—took the lead. She stormed through the tunnel, skidding to a halt with a shriek when the ground abruptly ended. The tunnel had spit them out at the edge of a massive cavern. Aris couldn't see the bottom, but across the pit was another narrow platform and another tunnel. As her eyes adjusted to the familiar blue glow, she realized there wasn't just one other platform, but several. She counted at least eight ahead, and who knows how many below, each connected by a set of stairs.

God, why did it have to be stairs?

By the time they'd reached the sixth flight, Aris felt the sweat soaking her thighs, the dampness of her jeans the only assurance that she had in fact made it out of the portal, and this wasn't just the hell people ended up in when they failed to cross over.

Seven flights. It was Mr. Matthews she thought of then, and what kind of hell he'd ended up in, or if he was somehow still alive.

Eight flights. Was what they'd done really any different from shooting him?

Nine flights. And then—*is that . . . sunlight?*

Not just sunlight. The sound of waves crashing, and the cry of seagulls scavenging for food. She swallowed a mouthful of salty air as Mirai bolted up the last stretch of steps. Then, a muffled scream followed by a shrill, "This is incredible!"

Aris wiped the sweat from her face. The cave opened onto some sort of beach. Nothing about it looked particularly magical, and yet, she couldn't shake the feeling it gave her.

This was it. This was exactly where they were meant to be.

She didn't have to look back to know the others were thinking the same thing, but she did anyway. She wanted to see it, not just feel it.

Wanted to see the looks on all their faces as they realized that the legend they'd been chasing was no longer just a dream.

The wonder she saw in their eyes was everything.

It was everything.

And then it was gone.

"Take them," a deep voice said, and Aris whirled to see who it came from. All she could see was a flurry of black cloaks.

Yuki stepped in front of Mirai, as if he'd chosen this moment to try out the defensive older brother routine. He probably thought he was being brave, but *stupid* was a better word for it. Mirai tugged him back with enough force to ensure he didn't try it again, just as Alek moved to shield Evie and Aris. He'd just planted a foot when Jada collapsed to the ground, muttering something Aris couldn't hear, and when she turned back, she saw Lochlen's long body unconscious in their arms.

Someone shouted, "Secure the prophet!" and Aris stepped forward to block Lochlen's body. A sharp pain burrowed between her eyes. Then she was on her knees.

The last thing she heard was someone bellow, "Send word to the Queen. Tell Her Majesty we've got the Seer." And then everything went black.

Pronunciation Guide

Lochlen Heresi .... LOCK-lin|HEH-ruh-see
[HE/HIM/HIS]

Aleksander Davenport ...a-luhk-ZAN-dr|DA-vuhn-port
[HE/HIM/HIS]

Aris .... EH-ruhs
[SHE/HER/HERS]

Mirai .... mr-EYE
[SHE/HER/HERS]

Yuki .... YOO-kee
[HE/HIM/HIS]

Jada .... JAY-duh
[ANY PRONOUNS]

Harrison Matthews .... harr-i-SUHN|MATH-yooz
[HE/HIM/HIS]

Evie .... eev-EE
[SHE/HER/HERS]

Garret .... geh-RUHT
[HE/HIM/HIS]

Braxton (Brax) .... BRAKS-tuhn (braks)
[HE/HIM/HIS]

Tuatha De Danann .... too-ah day don-an

Llewellyn .... loo-WEHL-ihn

Krysidia .... kri-SIHD-ee-uh

Krysidian .... kri-SIHD-ee-uhn

Anathemian .... a-nuh-THEE-mee-uhn

Gwirsiare .... gwir-see-AIR

Gwardyn .... WOR-dn

Elsley .... ELZ-lee

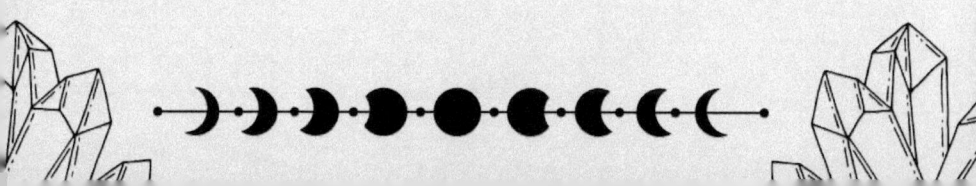

ACKNOWLEDGMENTS

This book has taken my heart, my soul, and quite possibly, my sanity—three things I never would have been willing to sacrifice if it weren't for the wonderful support and encouragement I received. Without my parents I never would have had the time, nor the stability to finish this story, and for that I owe them the world. Special thanks to my mother, for happily reading every draft I threw at her (even the bad ones). And to my father, thank you for using every resource at your disposal to answer my never-ending list of questions, and also for boasting about me to the rest of the family.

To Jess and Jordan, thanks for letting me word vomit all over you guys. Sometimes a good rant was all I needed to continue to push forward. And to Jen, you will forever be my bookish bestie. Thank you for hyping me up whenever I started losing steam. This story has been a long time coming, but your excitement has been pivotal in fueling the flame.

I owe a huge thanks to my editor, Brenna Bailey-Davies. You were a dream to work with, and I couldn't have asked for a better editor.

To my cover artist, Alice Maria Power, your work is stunning, and you absolutely nailed my vision for both the dust jacket, and the laminate cover.

To my proofreader, Elyssa, you have a killer attention to detail. Thanks for being my final pair of eyes.

I owe a special thanks to Heather Masters, my audiobook narrator, for bringing this book and all its characters to life.

Thank you to all the booksellers, librarians, teachers, and book bloggers who have already started to support the series.

To my beta readers. You were my lighthouse when I was lost in the fog.

I am so grateful to the rest of my family, for their continual love and support. You never once questioned my dreams or doubted my ability to achieve them.

To my oldest friends. Thank you for being there, and for holding on as long as you did. I owe you everything.

And finally, to you, the reader. Thank you for picking up this book. Thank you for giving this world and it's characters a chance.